L

Also by Rodney Hobson

Paul Amos murder mysteries:
(published as ebooks by Endeavour Press)

Unlikely Graves

Unholy Murder

Kith and Kill

The Hanging tree

Investment and finance books:
(Published by Harriman House)

Shares Made Simple

The Book of Scams

Understanding Company News

How to Build a Share Portfolio

The Dividend Investor

Small Companies, Big Profits

Dead Money

RODNEY HOBSON

© Rodney Hobson, 2013

Published by Rodney Hobson

First published as an ebook 2013 by Endeavour Press Ltd.

A CIP catalogue record for this book is available from the British Library.

ISBN 978-1-9998264-0-6

Book layout and design by Clare Brayshaw

Cover design by Michael Roscoe

Prepared and printed by:

York Publishing Services Ltd
64 Hallfield Road
Layerthorpe
York YO31 7ZQ

Tel: 01904 431213

Website: www.yps-publishing.co.uk

For Marie and Alex

Acknowledgements

I would like to thank Marie Hobson, Jackie Millar, Margaret Parker and Fiona Rodger for reading the original manuscript and suggesting improvements

Prologue

The dark came as a shock. It was obviously expected but there was no way of preparing for it, no way of practising for it.

Nor was there any going back. This might be the only opportunity and there was desperately little time.

The stairs were fairly easy, a regular height that could be taken with a steady step, touching the wall with the left hand to guide round corners. It was the level part at each floor and halfway up each flight that was tricky, the sudden lurch forward when the expected step up was missing.

Then came another shuffle round the corner until a toe end caught the next flight.

It was too risky to try counting the stairs. The important thing was to count the floors, to be sure of getting the right one. Two flat turns to each storey.

Heat from the day lingered on the stairway despite the darkness of the night. Heat, fear and exertion combined to create a cold sweat by the time the right floor was reached.

There was a thin light emanating from under one of the doors. That was much more frightening than the pitch blackness of the stairs. It was from the far left hand door, though, diagonally opposite, not the first on the right. Four doors to each floor, two on either side of the eight foot wide open space between the flats.

And that strip of light was just enough to show where the nearest door was for a pair of eyes that had grown accustomed to darkness. Enough light to avoid clanging the bar against the wall as it was swapped to the left hand and the key to the right, enough to find the keyhole with a shaking hand and to turn the key.

The door clinked slightly as it was opened but the chain was not on. The curtains were open and the crescent moon was on this side of the building yet it still took a few precious seconds to make out the way through the lounge, where the curtains had been left open, and into the short passage to the bedrooms.

Two doors were closed but the one at the far left of the passage was ajar. That had to be the right one. If it wasn't, then all might be lost.

The bedroom was dark but a dull glow from a digital bedside clock outlined just the vaguest of shapes. Luck was running, it was going to be all right.

Down came the bar with a grunt. A pause for breath, then another blow. Then another, the series building up into a frenzy, striking all over the bed to be sure.

Not a sound came from the shape. The bar fell noiselessly onto the thick carpet.

An elbow caught with a start against something at the side. Eyes that were slowly adjusting to what little light emanated from the digital clock made out a bedside lamp.

One click of the switch flooded the room with light to reveal the full horror of what had happened.

Chapter 1

"It's coming to something," grumbled Nick Foster as he brushed up the leaves. "Coming to something."

It's coming to something when you have to put a security barrier up, Foster thought. This is Lincolnshire in the 1990s, for heavens sake. Dull, quiet Lincolnshire. He stopped and looked round. There was no-one to grumble to out loud.

Foster was quite used to talking to himself. His own company was as good as anything else on offer.

Killiney Court was just a small block of flats in a small village – well, a fairly large block in a fairly large village by Lincolnshire standards, Foster muttered away to himself. Hardly Chicago in the 1930s.

Killiney Court used to be council property but years of neglect, thanks to a combination of uncaring tenants and a cash-strapped council, had led to a decision to bulldoze the place. Sleathorpe Properties stepped in at the last minute, picked the place up for a nominal sum and spent hundreds of thousands of pound on refurbishment.

Here was the result: 24 luxury flats, four to each floor, in a solid brick and concrete building. It was a lifestyle that was beyond the hope of most of the surrounding rural populace but even paradise has its price. Killiney Court had been beset by petty thieving. It had caused tension among the residents as well as complaints that it was easy for envious outsiders to get in.

Hence the new sentry box that was being erected across the entrance. There a guard could sit all day and night, the tedium broken only by occasionally swinging the barrier up and down to let cars in and out of the short narrow drive.

Grumble and rustle, rustle and grumble, Foster edged his way round the bottom of the block. He was the one who got all the blame for everything that went wrong, blame from a bunch of snooty outsiders who walked past him as if he wasn't there except when they had something to complain about.

He was in no rush. He was 70 and would die leaning on his broom, though he did not intend that to happen for a long time yet. He had looked 70 since he was 50 and would still look 70 when he was 90.

His hair, though grey, was mainly intact. His face was chubby but lined and showed the white stubble of two days without a shave. His body and clothes were indeterminate, as he hid them under an ill-fitting overall tied loosely at the waist.

He bore the hallmarks of a man who no longer had a wife to keep him up to scratch, no-one to make an effort for.

The ground level at Killiney Court was open except for the lift in the centre at the back.

"Wind blows right through," he chuntered. "Brings all the dirt and leaves. Now we've got the building mess as well."

Foster had a point. One workman was drilling into tarmac and concrete while another stood supervising. They were making rather more mess than was necessary. No one, however, paid much attention to Foster's grumbles, which were in any case directed mainly to himself.

Even the security guard, sitting at his temporary desk under the shelter of the block where he had taken up his duties at the beginning of the week, had learned to turn a deaf ear by the fifth day.

"Just keep an eye on things, Nick, while I nip to the toilet," he said, easing off the chair and ambling round behind the lifts in the opposite direction to the portable toilet sited discretely in a corner to avoid offending the susceptible eyes of the residents.

"Toilets aren't that way," Foster grumbled to himself. He knew the guard was going for a cigarette. Smoking on duty was a serious sin, a sackable offence. Some of the hoity toity residents didn't like to return to their palatial mansions to be confronted by a security guard with a cigarette protruding from his mouth, forcing them to run the gauntlet of a ring of smoke.

That was the fifth time the guard had "gone to the toilet" and it was still only midday.

"Friday the thirteenth," grumbled Foster. Rustle and grumble. "Unlucky for somebody."

It was 4.30 pm when the first car drove in and the new barrier was raised in earnest for its debut performance. Ray Jones, local businessman, entrepreneur with a finger in a dozen small-time enterprises dotted around the area, steered his BMW towards the barrier. He could afford a Mercedes, he told himself frequently, and others occasionally, but he did not like to display his wealth.

Jones, late fifties, stocky, heavily greying and slightly round-shouldered, waved peremptorily at the lone sentinel, now half way through his allotted shift and seated proudly, if a little uncomfortably, in his bright new sentry box. He pressed a button and the barrier swung up, just a little too late to avoid forcing Jones to slow almost to a halt.

Jones gave him a sharp look that meant "get the timing right", then he swung away into his parking slot down the left hand side of the block and under the high surrounding wall. As he got out and clicked the remote control key to lock the car, he heard a loud peep from another vehicle following him in.

The second car *was* a Mercedes. Scott Warren's signal had alerted the guard, who this time swung up the barrier far too soon. This incident annoyed Jones twice over: he hated people to misuse their horns and that guard, who would have to be paid out of the community fees, had got the timing on the barrier wrong again. Jones liked things in their proper place at their proper times just as God had intended them.

"Evening, Ray," Warren called cheerily from his open window as he drove past to his own bay two further on. Jones stood and watched the younger man with a mixture of contempt and annoyance.

The parking bays had been allocated all wrong, Jones thought. Why was nothing done properly these days? He and Warren were in adjoining flats yet their parking bays were not adjoining. It was very irritating.

He waited until Warren was getting out of the car and was caught in that awkward position with the door open, one leg out on the ground and one still in the well in front of the seat – the momentary pause before the driver summons the extra ounce of energy to rise to his feet.

"Christian names are for Christians," Jones remarked bluntly, "and horns are for warning other road users, not for greeting all and sundry."

Warren gave just a hint of being put out by this rebuke, then he sprang to his feet with a forced laugh. He was 30 years younger, tall, fit, well built and still tanned from a late summer holiday.

"What an old fusspot you are, Ray," he returned, deliberately using the familiar tone of address that he knew irked Jones. "What do they teach you at church on a Sunday night? Hate thy neighbour? Don't be so stuffy. It's all first names now."

Yet for all his bluster, Warren was clearly the lesser of the two men and both knew it.

There is a thin line between smugness and charisma and Jones was on the right side of it. He had a presence that Warren would never have, especially now Warren was struggling to fabricate the natural air that had come so readily when he and Jones had first met.

Warren ran one of those newfangled high tech operations that Jones fervently believed would never really catch on: his own small video recording company. Despite his reservations, Jones had finally agreed to back it financially, driving a hard bargain and hoping for a quick profit before the fad inevitably died a natural death or technology moved on.

Warren had shown a bit more respect then, when he needed the money. All that equipment was expensive and Jones had slowly turned the screw until Warren was finally reduced to grovelling for it.

Still, the operation had started to make its mark. Warren had contacts in London, from where most of the work emanated – work that could be done anywhere in the country, whizzed down high speed telephone wires or delivered in bubble wrapped packages by express couriers. The investment was beginning to come good and Jones had finally got a small dividend. It was a start, but not enough and not quickly enough.

The two men walked together nearly to the lift, side by side but a good yard apart. The awkwardness was broken when Jones spotted a third vehicle approaching down Killiney Road. As the car turned into the drive, the barrier swung up, nicely timed so that the Ford Mondeo eased through without having to change speed. The guard was getting the hang of it.

Joanna Stevens was a tall, handsome woman in her early 30s, as was readily apparent when she stepped from her car, which she parked on the opposite side from the two men. Warren hesitated and watched as Jones strode across to her.

Warren disliked the woman intensely but viewed her with trepidation. She was a jumped up little brat who interfered too much, who thought she knew it all but who hadn't the guts to drive a sports car. She dressed old for her age, too. Yet he almost feared her, for her command of figures was quite awesome and he was obliged to put his books at her mercy because Jones insisted on it as a condition of his investment.

Jones, on the other hand, held Stevens in great respect, as a person as well as a business consultant. She had saved him from one or two dubious investments and brought into line those company owners who thought they could take his money and do what they liked with it. Jones admired her choice of car, too: like him, she drove a less expensive vehicle than she could afford, avoiding attention by not flaunting her status.

Warren strained to hear what was being said but Jones spoke in low tones until the heathen videoman, as Jones called him behind his back, gave up and took the lift that had stood open and waiting for him for several seconds. The conversation between Jones and Stevens was, though, as Warren feared.

"Next week I want you to crawl through Warren's books," Jones said quietly but deliberately. "I think he is concealing something serious."

"You think he is hiding profits from you?" Stevens replied, more as a statement than a question.

"That, or he is in big trouble and manufactured this year's profit to appease me. I suspect the latter."

Steven nodded her agreement as they walked towards the lift that Warren had taken up. It had returned already. Warren must have considerately pressed the ground floor button as he vacated it, probably hoping that the lift's reappearance would cut short the conversation. Stevens and Jones moved towards it in silence. Foster leaned on his brush and watched. The security guard was sitting in his booth, watching the others out of sheer boredom.

It was the last time that anyone was prepared to admit to having seen the victim alive.

Chapter 2

The closing hymn at the compact parish church lacked something of its usual fervour that Sunday evening. Sarah Miles, the organist, normally picked the hymns. It was one job fewer for the vicar to do, so he was happy to delegate the task.

The Day Thou Gavest, Lord, is Ended was Ray Jones's favourite hymn but Miles could see, in the little mirror giving her a view of the congregation, the space that he usually occupied religiously remained empty.

She glanced several times into her mirror during the service as if to contradict what her eyes had already seen over and over again. It was rare, indeed, for Jones to miss Sunday evensong. Not even business prevented his ritual appearance.

Miles had seen Jones on Friday morning in Horncastle and he had remarked casually as they parted: "See you on Sunday."

Miles pulled out the oboe stop instead of the cor anglais. Flustered, she selected a 32ft pipe instead of a 16ft, giving the tune a deeper tone. She always played the hymn as Jones wanted it, as a celebration of the day; now it sounded like a requiem for the ending of it.

"Don't worry so," the Rev John Thornley told her after the service. "I'm sure Mr Jones was held up on some unexpected business. You did tell me he was going to Nottingham earlier today, as I recall."

He did not wish to be rude to Miles – her services as an organist were too valuable to him – but she did fuss over nothing. She was 50, and if anything looked older. Had she been in her teens people would have thought her anorexic.

Thornley was not anxious to get involved in a conversation appertaining to Raymond Jones. Miles could blow hot and cold on any topic, particularly so where Jones was concerned.

Thornley had no doubts about his organist's feelings for Jones. She doted on him, mainly from afar – not in distance but in minds.

As far as he knew, Miles had never been in love, or if she had it had come to nothing. There had never been any mention, not even the merest hint, of a former boyfriend – not that Thornley was particularly interested. He regarded prying into other people's love lives as rather prurient, not far short of a sin.

Still, you couldn't help being a bit interested, especially the way that Sarah Miles had clung to Ray Jones like a limpet after his wife left him.

She gave Jones a sympathetic ear over a cup of coffee at the little cafes in Horncastle. She took him to the occasional concert in Lincoln, thus giving Jones a new insight into the music that had been her life. She made a great effort to smarten herself up with fashionable clothes so she could accompany him to the occasional social function held by businessmen in the county.

In short, Miles had come alive.

The same could not, strictly speaking, be said for Ray Jones. He liked Sarah Miles, they got on well and he always treated her with great courtesy in a rather old-fashioned way. Some parishioners, heaven forgive them, rather despised Miles; Jones most certainly did not.

But Jones's side of the relationship lacked passion. He clearly saw Miles as a friend but no more.

Perhaps, Thornley wondered, that was what added the intensity to the relationship. Miles was content to be no more than friends provided it was best friends. She would hover close by, simmering gently, if he spoke to any of the other females after church service. She would simmer not so gently if she did not see him for several days.

"Vicar."

Thornley was brought back to reality by the insistent voice in his ear. He shook his head involuntarily.

Miles had already virtually cleared the church by the simple expedient of playing the Hallelujah Chorus on full organ as the closing voluntary. It was her time honoured method, on the odd occasions when she wanted to get away quickly, of discouraging the little knots of people who gathered in the aisle after evensong, enjoying a musical accompaniment to their gossip.

Finding no sympathy with the vicar, she bustled off to her home just 100 yards away from the gate. Miles rang Jones breathlessly as soon as she was through the door, without even removing her hat, the one she always wore to church because Ray had helped her to choose it.

The rather flat voice belonging to the object of her concern answered on the fourth ring.

"This is Ray Jones. Please leave a message stating your name, your number and when you rang. This computer occasionally crashes, wiping out voice messages, so if I don't respond please ring again tomorrow."

"Raymond, it's Sarah. Where on earth are you? It's not like you to miss evensong. I'm worried sick about you. Ring me whatever time you get back."

But Jones did not ring back that evening. Miles tried again at 9 pm, and then again at 2 am when she woke from her fitful sleep. Each time she left a similar but increasingly frantic message in vain.

She woke with a start on Monday morning. It was 9.30 am. She would normally have been awake for the past two hours. She rang Jones's office. No, he had not been in yet but that was nothing unusual. He would call in during the day and they would let him know that she had rung.

Miles left another message on the answering machine installed on the computer in Jones's flat. Perhaps the wretched machine had crashed and he had not got her messages. That afternoon there was still no sign of Jones.

Finally Miles rang Jones's housekeeper.

"I'm due in tomorrow morning," she responded. "I'll be there at ten o'clock."

No, she wasn't prepared to go round that evening.

Miles begged, pleaded, cajoled. Frantically she began to threaten the unyielding housekeeper, who finally realised there was to be no reasoning with the infatuated woman and put down the phone.

Miles rang the police. No, they were not going to break in. They followed their customary method of discouraging persistent callers by leaving the phone lying on the desk while they got on with their paperwork until the sound of the voice at the other end ceased abruptly.

That was why the body of Raymond Jones, businessman, entrepreneur, finger-in-every-pie man and staunch churchgoer, was not found until Tuesday morning.

Chapter 3

Detective Inspector Paul Amos dreaded the smell of death, and it hung over Ray Jones's flat 6A, Killiney Court, that sunny Tuesday morning. Jones lay in the bed, his skull crushed, dried blood covering the pillows. A rusty iron bar lay on the floor.

There was only one dip in the pillows on the double bed and that was occupied by Jones's severely damaged head.

"He's been dead some time, three or four days," pathologist Brian Slater remarked gloomily. Slater hated his job but there was nothing else he was any good at so he was stuck with it.

"Looks like he was struck several times. This was a frenzied attack. They made a right mess."

Amos cursed his luck. He had been tied up with the Chief Constable on some new road safety campaign when word of the murder reached headquarters and had made the 20 mile journey east from Lincoln after Slater and Detective Sergeant Juliet Swift had beaten him to it. Now he was playing catch-up.

"Would you say it was likely to be a man to strike such heavy blows?" Amos enquired.

"Could easily have been a woman," was Slater's opinion, "and not necessarily a strong one at that. If she caught Jones sleeping she wouldn't have needed to hit him hard. Just often."

Swift was organising a detailed examination of the apartment.

"There's no sign of a break-in, Sir," she told Amos. "Either the intruder had a key or Jones let him in."

"He?" asked Amos.

"This is a man's work," Swift commented curtly.

"Jones looks to have been asleep when he was attacked," Amos continued as if ignoring her remark. "So either he let the killer in then went to bed with her – or him," he added in appeasement to the sergeant, "or the killer had a key.

"There's no second dent in the bed so the latter seems more likely."

"His housekeeper, Jan Morris, has one," said Swift. "She came in at ten this morning, her usual time. Some woman called Sarah Miles was with her. She was in a right old flap. She was the one who found Jones's body. She says she doesn't have a key – that's why she came in with the housekeeper."

"What do you mean, that's why she came in with the housekeeper? Why did she come at all? Was Jones expecting her?"

"No, she says she was worried about him. She was a bit hysterical. I gather he never missed evensong at the local church unless he was on holiday. When he didn't turn up on Sunday she kept ringing him. He wasn't at work yesterday, either. Oh, and she keeps going on about the police not doing their job. Something about refusing to break the door down."

Amos wandered over to the bedside light, which was switched on. He touched the bulb and withdrew his hand sharply. It was very hot.

Swift butted in: "The bedside light was on, Sir, when the two women came in. They say the main light was off and the curtains were closed. We opened them so we could see what we were doing."

Amos nodded to Swift and she closed the curtains. The inspector then switched off the ceiling light. It was quite dark. The bulb in the bedside light was only 40 watts.

Nonetheless, the attacker would have been able to see Jones distinctly if dimly. Satisfied, Amos switched the main light on and Swift opened the curtains again.

Amos was apparently losing interest in Sarah Miles, who had been taken downstairs and put in a police car under the consoling supervision of a female uniformed constable to allow unfettered access to the various rooms in the flat.

There was a framed photograph of a younger man in a suit and a woman in a wedding dress lying on the floor, apparently having been knocked off the bedside table, either intentionally or by accident. The glass was cracked.

The inspector edged out into the short corridor that ran from the living room to the bedrooms and pushed open a door that was only fractionally ajar. His eyes were wandering to the telephone point in what had originally been intended as a second bedroom but had been converted by Jones into a home office.

"Where's the answering machine?" he asked. "Surely Jones would have one."

It was a young constable who supplied the information: "The phone's linked into the computer, Sir. It's on screensaver at the moment."

Before Amos, who had no idea what screensaver was, had a chance to tell the junior officer to speak English, the lad touched the mouse and the computer whirred into life.

"This is top bananas!" he called out appreciatively.

A coupled of clicks and the screen proclaimed two old messages and six new ones. The unreliable software had not crashed.

"I'll play the old messages first, the ones Jones had listened to," suggested the constable.

Amos grunted assent.

They were a couple of calls from Jones's office, made the previous week and merely confirming business meetings. The new messages were more interesting.

The first was a man's voice: "Look, Ray, can we have a quick word over the weekend. I'm sure we can sort out whatever's bothering you. I'll pop over to see you this afternoon. No need to involve Joanna."

Then a woman: "It's Joanna. I've been thinking about what you said. You could be right. I'm in Scunthorpe on Monday but I'll drop in unannounced first thing Tuesday. Don't worry, I'll have a good excuse."

Then followed four increasingly frantic messages from Sarah Miles, each meticulously stating who she was, the time of her call and her phone number.

"Get them transcribed," Amos ordered. "Computers have a habit of losing things."

He moved on through the apartment.

"We've spoken to the caretaker," Swift said. "He says Killiney Court is built in an octagonal with four flats on each floor. They are identical except they are grouped in pairs that are a mirror image of each other.

"The flats are numbered according to the floor they are on. The first flat on the right as you come out of the lift is A like this one and the others are lettered round anti-clockwise to D."

Amos raised his eyebrows.

"I thought clockwise was the natural order of things," he said drily.

"Apparently the floors were numbered clockwise when the council owned the building but the new private owners wanted to change everything," Swift replied.

Amos nodded that he understood.

There were two bedrooms, a lounge, a bathroom, a shower, a separate toilet and a kitchen. Outside the kitchen was an open laundry area.

Amos looked out of the laundry. The outside was like a large window with no glass. Directly opposite was a similar arrangement for the other flat in the pair, 6B.

That's a third way in, he remarked to Sgt Swift. "I reckon a fit young man or woman with sufficient nerve – or sufficiently desperate – could jump across that gap. I think we had better have a list of all the residents in this block. We shall have to interview them all.

"And I shall start with whoever lives in that flat opposite."

Chapter 4

The owner of flat 6B was not conveniently at home, as persistent ringing of the doorbell ascertained.

Amos and Swift made their way down to the dark mezzanine floor where caretaker Nick Foster occupied a small flat squeezed into the space at the back of the block.

Foster eagerly supplied the information that Scott Warren ran the Ace Plus Video recording studio in Gainsborough Road, Horncastle, and that he had indeed left the block as usual that morning.

Any thoughts that a guilty murderer was hiding behind the locked door of flat 6B were thus assuaged, though Foster did take the opportunity of relating and embroidering the arrival at the block of Ray Jones, Scott Warren and Joanna Stevens the previous Friday.

Foster remained half hidden behind his partly open door, holding it firmly in place, until the two officers started to move away, when he finally relaxed to come partly out onto the landing and offer advice on the best route to the recording studio.

"Did you get the impression that the caretaker was trying to get rid of us?" Amos asked Swift as they descended in the lift.

Swift agreed: "He was certainly keen enough to make out that Warren and Jones had a stand-up row on Friday evening when they arrived back at Killiney Court."

It was only as they emerged from the lift at the ground floor that Amos realised to his horror that he had completely forgotten about the two women who had found the body. He had been so intent on inspecting the flat before it was disturbed and then was distracted by the thought of confronting the first obvious suspect that he had put everything else out of his mind.

His first reaction to Sarah Miles and the housekeeper was that they were innocent victims, two women with little or nothing to connect them apart from the dead man, two women who had the misfortune to turn up at the wrong place at the wrong time.

They were now sitting patiently and silently, looking shell-shocked, in the back seat of a marked police vehicle.

Common sense dictated that the two women should be interviewed separately so their stories could be crosschecked for anomalies. People confronted by the same sight can remember the events differently, especially when the sight is a nasty shock.

However, Amos was particularly anxious to find Scott Warren, a man who had exchanged cross words with the murdered man and who potentially had access to his flat by an unorthodox route hidden from view.

While it was not politic to alienate the two women, Amos did not want to waste too much time on them before pursuing his main quarry.

"Let's just have a quick chat with them, Juliet," the inspector said to Swift as they approached the vehicle. "Get a quick impression then send them home in a police car to recover from the shock and say we will talk to them later."

Swift said nothing. She didn't really approve of treating the women casually but she agreed that Warren needed to be accosted at the earliest opportunity.

A uniformed police officer sat in the driver's seat. Amos opened the front passenger door and half sat in the seat with his legs still outside the car.

"Ladies," he said sympathetically. "We won't keep you much longer after your ordeal and thank you for your forbearance. I just want you to tell me why you were here entering Mr Jones's flat this morning and, if you can, what you saw."

Sarah Miles was much the keener of the two women to speak.

"I told the Horncastle police we needed to act," she burst forth with a vengeance. "But would they act? Oh, no."

"Miss Miles," Amos cut in before she could build up to a flood. "Your complaint about the police I will look into in due course when I can give it all the attention it deserves."

Swift's intake of breath, outside the car, was mercifully not audible to Miles in the rear seat. Miles, however, failed to notice the double-edged nature of Amos's assurance.

"Why were you so worried about Mr Jones that you came here this morning?" Amos asked.

Miles scowled.

"Raymond never missed evensong on Sunday – not unless he had good reason to be away," she said. "It was obvious something was wrong. He didn't answer his phone. He didn't turn up at his office yesterday. How much more reason do you want?"

"You're a friend of Mr Jones?" Amos asked.

"Yes," Miles said emphatically.

"Forgive me, Miss Miles, but I have to ask if it was more than friendship. Were you and Mr Jones an item?"

Sarah Miles snorted.

"Mr Jones and I were very close," she said deliberately. "Very close. He was a dear, dear man, loyal and generous to his friends. He was devastated after his wife left him. I helped him to pick up the pieces.

"But it was no more than that," she added hurriedly.

"Do you know where his wife is now?" Amos asked.

Miles shook her head and lapsed into silence.

"And you're Mr Jones's housekeeper," Amos said to the other woman. No-one had mentioned her name and she seemed quite anonymous next to the more loquacious Miles.

"Yes," came the dull reply. "I am."

"How often did you come in?"

"Two days a week, Tuesdays and Thursdays. Mr Jones was never any trouble," she added with a catch in her voice.

"So you entered the flat fearing that something was wrong?"

"I did, she didn't," Miles butted in. "Nobody took me seriously. But I know Raymond better than anyone else – and now unfortunately I've proved it."

"So, you came into the flat," Amos said. "Did everything look normal?"

"In the lounge, yes," Miles replied. Having been done out of her rant against the police she was not to be deprived of centre stage in relating what had happened. Not that the housekeeper seemed inclined to say any more than necessary.

"We looked in the kitchen and laundry but found nothing untoward. Then we went down the corridor to the other rooms.

"I wouldn't normally have been so presumptuous," she added hastily, "had I not feared for Raymond. The first door along was a study and he wasn't there. So we peeped into his bedroom and there he was …"

Miles tailed off as the horror of what they discovered came pouring back to her.

"I'm sorry to have to ask this," Amos said, "but who actually found Mr Jones?"

"I did," the housekeeper finally spoke, without emotion. "I could see from the door that a light was on so I knocked first then went in."

"You would obviously know the layout of the flat," Amos said to the housekeeper, "but did you, Miss Miles?"

"Of course not," she retorted indignantly. "I'd been in the lounge, of course, in the past but that was all. My relationship with Raymond wasn't like that."

Amos decided not to ask what "that" meant. Instead, he asked: "So you didn't go straight to the bedroom where he was found?"

Miles merely shook her head.

"This officer will take you home," the inspector said quietly. "Do either of you want someone to stay with you?"

Both women declined.

"Take a note of their addresses," Amos told the officer in the driver's seat.

Then to the women he said: "We will almost certainly want to talk to you further but I think that for now you have been through enough. This officer will see you safely home."

As the barrier rose to allow the police car to pull out of Killiney Court, Swift said to her superior officer: "I'm sorry, Sir, but we should have talked to them separately. Their reactions were completely different."

Amos looked at the detective sergeant in surprise.

"How do you mean," he asked.

"The housekeeper was shocked, yes – that's understandable as she was the one who actually found the body – but there was no emotion in her face. I'll bet that Jones was just an employer and no more. She can soon find another one."

Amos was interested now.

"And Sarah Miles?"

"That was personal. She was upset for Jones personally. I'm sure they were more than friends. I'd like to talk to the housekeeper to ask how Miles reacted, from entering the flat to finding the body."

Amos thought for a moment.

"You think that she could be a jealous lover? If she was, it would make sense for her to have been there on Friday night."

"And if things turned nasty," Swift said, "and she flew into a rage and killed him then the frantic efforts to gain admission to his flat in company with someone else over the weekend, and the messages on his answer machine, could have been a cover."

Chapter 5

The two officers had some difficulty locating the studios in the north west corner of Horncastle. There was no sign outside. Scott Warren was not interested in attracting passing trade.

Eventually they located a door round the side of a building and pressed an unmarked intercom button.

A few seconds later a terse voice responded curtly: "Yes?"

Amos introduced himself and Swift without specifying the reason for their visit.

"Is this urgent? I'm very busy," the disembodied voice responded unhelpfully.

"Yes it is," Amos replied equally curtly. "Or do we need to get a search warrant?"

This was probably an empty threat, Amos thought to himself, but it didn't sound empty and a buzzer indicated that the door had been released.

As the two officers entered, a light topped by a multi-coloured lampshade came on at the top of the staircase running up from the door. The walls had been painted in a wide variety of blocks of clashing colours. Amos wondered if this was a tribute to Picasso's Cubism or a means of eliminating the cost of decorating by eking out the remains left in paint tins used on walls elsewhere.

Warren received them anxiously. His initial perturbation at the mention of Jones's name, however, gave way to apparent relief when Swift informed him that it was a murder investigation.

"No, we didn't have a blazing row on Friday evening," he responded to a question from Swift. The curtness had vanished and Warren was growing in cockiness and geniality in equal measure.

"Who told you that?" he asked expansively, spreading his arms wide in a gesture of openness. "We happened to arrive home at the same time and exchanged a few civil words. Ray Jones invested in my firm. I needed his cash to set up and he needed my expertise to produce a profit.

"He's invested in dozens of businesses in this town – and further afield. Some were more successful than others. Mine was among his better choices."

So what had Warren done since that civil conversation, Amos wondered out loud.

"It was about quarter to five when I left Jones talking to Joanna Stevens. She's his nosey parker accountant. She lives in the block two floors directly below Jones at 4A. You want to talk to her. I reckon Jones was making unwelcome advances to her. Maybe he went a bit too far."

"Your movements since Friday teatime," Amos prompted him.

"I did a bit of paperwork, tidied up the week's accounts, then I stuck in some oven chips and grilled a chop. I went down to the pub, had a couple of pints and a few games of darts with the usual crowd, and got back to the flat about 11.30 pm.

"I always have a lie-in on Saturday mornings and play squash in the afternoon. I took a girl friend out in the evening – I can give you the name of the restaurant – saw her home and got back latish on.

"Sunday I read the newspapers. It takes most of the day to get through the heavies. In the evening I had three friends round to play bridge until quite late."

"I shall need the names of the people you say you have been with," Amos interjected.

Warren hesitated for several seconds. Finally he replied reluctantly: "I can give you the names, of course, but I'd rather you didn't approach them unless you really have to. I don't greatly like the idea of my friends knowing that I've been interviewed in a murder inquiry. Especially the young lady."

"You live alone, I take it?" Swift said to keep the pressure on Warren while he had the threat of telling his girlfriend he was a murder suspect hanging over him.

Warren nodded.

"So for large chunks of the weekend you were in the flat on your own?"

"So was Joanna Stevens," he ventured by way of a reply. "You should talk to her."

"We shall talk to all the Killiney Court residents," Amos said sharply. He was annoyed at being told how to do his job and doubly annoyed because Stevens was the next person he intended to interview anyway.

Nor was he best pleased when Warren added brightly: "You're in luck. Here she is now."

Chapter 6

Amos and Swift followed Warren's gaze out through the window behind them. They could see a woman climbing out of a car and heading across the small car park at the rear of the building towards the outer door on the ground floor where a few minutes earlier the officers had sought admission.

Warren squeezed out while the officers were momentarily distracted and pressed the buzzer to release the door. Moments later footsteps were heard on the stairs.

Half way up, Joanna Stevens spotted Scott Warren standing at his office door at the top of the flight.

"Good morning, Scott," she called out brightly. "Just a routine VAT tidying up. I needn't bother you. I know where the books are."

She felt slightly suspicious that Warren was taking her arrival with aplomb. She had expected him to be nervous if, as she believed, he had something to hide.

"No time for that now," Warren answered cheerfully. "These people want to talk to you first."

Stevens was becoming increasingly perplexed. Warren was certainly good at escaping under a cloak of confusion.

"VAT inspectors?" she asked with a frown. "I thought I knew everyone at the Lincoln office."

"Police officers," Warren replied deliberately.

Stevens glanced at the occupants of the small office. Had the police found out about something more serious than she suspected? Embezzlement, perhaps? Why was he looking so complacent? Had he blamed her as the accountant?"

Warren was clearly amused at her discomfort.

"It concerns our mutual friend," he went on.

There was no flicker of understanding in Stevens' face.

"Whatever you have to discuss, I'm sure you can manage perfectly well without me," she said, flustered. The woman began backing out of the door.

"You left your flat early this morning, I take it?" Amos asked.

Stevens nodded.

"Perhaps you had better sit down. We have rather a shock for you."

Warren pushed forward his own chair with a slightly exaggerated gesture of gallantry that allowed him to take possession of the doorway, as if he were preparing to make a run for it. Stevens, however, remained standing, although she leaned against the wall for support.

Swift took up the explanation: "It concerns your neighbour and, we take it, business associate Raymond Jones. I'm sorry to have to tell you that he is dead. His body was found this morning. He had been murdered."

Stevens gasped audibly. Amos was torn between which of the two possible suspects to pursue first. Although annoyed that the flow of his interview with Warren had been interrupted, he decided it might be best at this stage to make a preliminary interrogation of Stevens, especially as she might throw some light on Warren's activities.

So he said: "Perhaps there is a spare room where we could have a quiet chat. As you know, Mr Jones lived in the same block of flats as yourself and you may have important evidence that could help us."

Stevens had recovered her composure.

"Do I take it, then," she asked, "that you don't yet know who killed him?"

"I keep an open mind," Amos replied.

Warren, ever eager to oblige in deflecting attention to Stevens, butted in again: "You can use my interview room. It's small but there's a table and a few chairs. Can I offer you some coffee?" he asked sweetly of the other occupants of his room.

"This way," said Steven curtly. "I know where it is. Let's get this done quickly."

Then to Warren: "No coffee for me."

Amos and Swift also declined.

They went through an internal door, the bottom half padded and the top half thick glass. It would deaden sound but allow anyone on the outside to peer in and avoid disturbing any recording session.

The interview room was the only other space in what passed for Scott Warren's business establishment. It was larger than the office they had just vacated but somewhat cramped with various pieces of electronic equipment and other paraphernalia of his trade.

Ensconced in the interview room, Amos asked Stevens when she had last seen the dead man.

"On Friday. It must have been just before 5 pm. Maybe a bit later. I drove into Killiney Court – as you apparently already know, I live there – and Ray and Warren were making their way to the lift. Ray broke off when he saw me and came over for a few words as I parked."

"Did you get the impression that Jones and Warren were falling out over something?"

"Not at all. Ray gets a bit flushed in the face when he is angry. He was perfectly calm."

"What did he say to you?"

"It was just some work he wanted me to do," Stevens said unhelpfully.

"Not personal?" Amos persisted.

"Are you trying to imply something?" Stevens asked coldly.

"You call Mr Jones 'Ray' and Mr Warren 'Warren'. I am bound to enquire, therefore, if your relationship with Mr Jones went beyond work."

"No it didn't. I just knew Ray – Mr Jones – better. I'd known him longer. And he was altogether a pleasanter person than Warren."

Apparently the video wizard was not going to get a handle to his name.

Amos felt inclined to push the personal angle: "Perhaps Mr Jones felt otherwise. Perhaps he pressed his attentions."

The colour was rising in Joanna Stevens' face but she was visibly controlling her anger. She's a cool customer, Amos thought.

"Ray was a business contact. I did a lot of work for him. He was also a not particularly close friend. And I mean, not particularly close."

"But he was on his own, his wife had left him, he was fancy free."

Stevens laughed.

"Ray didn't fancy his chances with me. I suppose Warren has been telling you this to take attention away from himself."

"And did the work Jones wanted doing have any bearing on your visit today?" Amos ventured with the benefit of the messages on Jones's answering machine.

"This is just a routine check of the books for the quarterly VAT return."

"I think it's rather more than that," Amos persisted. "You think Warren is cooking the books, don't you?"

Stevens was visibly taken aback to discover how well informed Amos clearly was so early in the investigation.

Then it dawned on her: "I take it Ray did not listen to the message I left for him on his answer machine. Or if he did, he didn't erase it. Well, I don't assume anything without evidence. I'm here at Ray's request to check if everything is in order."

Something she had seen through the window in the door of the room caused her to say suddenly: "Does it occur to you that while we are talking here Warren is covering his tracks?"

She rose as she uttered these words and her voice rose, too. "The sooner I get hold of the books, the better."

Stevens swept out of the room in search of the errant Warren.

"She's probably right," Amos conceded to Swift with a shrug of his shoulders. "We'd better have the crime squad look at his books as well."

The two officers followed Stevens. They found her back in Warren's private office surveying the cause of her disquiet.

A shredding machine that had been standing unnoticed in a corner had been moved quietly up to Warren's desk. He was standing with a smirk over a pile of shredded papers cascading onto his feet.

Chapter 7

Amos determined to discover as soon as possible what evidence if any Jones had for suspecting Warren was up to no good. It was just a 10 minute drive to Jones's office, where Amos and Swift found the office manageress, Jade Nolan, attempting to keep the wheels of business rolling.

It was a more prominent office than Warren's, located in the town centre looking across the cobbled market place and with a gleaming brass name plate bearing the legend "Ray Jones Enterprises".

It was, however, no larger than Warren's, comprising a front office, a back office, a toilet and a small kitchen where staff could make a brew or microwave lunch.

There were just two staff members, Nolan and a young assistant who looked about 13 to Amos but who was at least three years older assuming that she had left school. Neither showed any surprise when Amos identified himself and Swift.

"Yes, we've heard," Nolan said flatly. "We've heard."

Amos was astonished that news had travelled so quickly. Never mind, it was always something of a relief not to have to break bad news.

The young assistant was busy typing letters as the officers arrived but was happy to break off from what was a painstaking process. Her boss's computer at home might have been "top bananas" but the inexperienced assistant had to make do with a standard Remington typewriter.

The news evidently meant far less to her than it did to Nolan, whose eyes were glazed and who kept shuffling papers aimlessly on her own desk.

"Perhaps we could go through to the back," Amos suggested gently, eyeing the empty room through the half open door. "Then we won't be disturbed if anyone comes in."

Jade Nolan led the way through unenthusiastically, remarking only that "I suppose the vultures will be coming in."

She did, though, pause at the doorway and tell her assistant to brew some tea. Amos was about to decline but the teenager leapt up with enthusiasm. Her talents for tea brewing probably exceeded her skills at typing.

"I have to ask you, Miss Nolan," Amos said, taking the lack of a ring on her left hand as an indication that she was not a Mrs, "Whether you can think of anyone who might have wanted to harm Mr Jones."

"Not to kill him," Nolan said indignantly, suddenly coming to life. "Mr Jones was a very fair man. Firm, yes, but he had to be. He was in business. But he never actually shut anyone down. He went in and helped them if anyone was struggling. He would even take the business over and sell it for what he could raise rather than close it down."

This sounded to Amos like a recipe for making enemies. Stealing other people's businesses, if that was what he sometimes did, was hardly more endearing than foreclosing on a loan.

However, he did not want to pursue the point at this stage. There would be time to go through the rest of his books in due course.

Instead, he asked: "Did he have any business dealings with anyone at Killiney Court where he lived?"

"Only Mr Warren at the Ace Plus studios as far as I know," Nolan replied, "but of course I would know the investments from their business addresses so it's just possible there were others. It's a very prestigious address, you know, Killiney Court."

"Indeed, so I believe," Amos remarked.

"I only knew Mr Warren lived there because he came into the office once and he was very boastful about sharing the same address as such a respectable and successful businessman as Mr Jones."

At this point the young assistant brought in two beakers of tea which she set down unceremoniously in front of the two officers.

"I'll just get yours, Jade," she said.

"No need," Amos butted in quickly. Then to Nolan he said: "If you could kindly let us have Mr Warren's file we can let you get on with your work while we look through it."

She produced Warren's documents with some reluctance and allowed the police officers to take possession of Jones's personal office with even less enthusiasm. The fact that they were not, apparently, about to remove the documents partly assuaged her.

Amos opened the file and saw immediately that Jones had put £500,000 into the venture.

He looked for Nolan. She was slipping out back to the main office quietly but he caught her before the door closed.

"Tell me," he asked, "what sort of sums did Mr Jones usually invest in businesses?"

Nolan hesitated.

"It varied," she finally said. "Some businesses were bigger than others. It could be £20,000, it could be £100,000.

It depended on how much the business needed and how much Mr Jones had available for new investments at the time.

"He turned a lot of people down, you know. Mr Jones had a shrewd business brain. He didn't just invest in anything."

She was evidently fiercely proud off her late employer. She stopped short.

"Oh," she said looking at the file in Amos's hands.

"Yes, oh," replied the officer. "Mr Jones seems to have put rather more into this one. £500,000 worth, in fact."

Amos raised his eyebrows to indicate that he expected an answer.

"Certainly that was more than Mr Jones usually invested but Mr Warren managed to persuade him that his business had great potential. You can see that he produced correspondence from business contacts in London interested in using its services. His bank references were very good. So were his references from former employers.

"There are copies of everything in there. I'll leave you to it," she concluded and exited abruptly.

"She's very defensive," Amos remarked quietly once Nolan had closed the door.

"It's more than that," Swift commented. "She has the same wistful look in her eyes that Sarah Miles had whenever Ray Jones's name is mentioned – even if she does always refer to him as Mr Jones. This man must have had some charm, or charisma, or something."

"Hmmm," Amos said. "That supports the point you raised earlier that this could be a crime of passion rather than the work of an angry businessman."

Amos opened the file, scanning down the pages and passing them to Swift. The references were certainly good – a bit too good if anything. It was as if people were giving Warren references just to get rid of him.

These London business contacts, too. Their letters seemed to be offering work to Warren's studio but when you looked at them carefully they really amounted to very little. No-one was committed to anything. Surely Jones, hard-headed businessman that he was, had not committed so much money to such a risky venture.

"Perhaps Jones was just like the rest of us," Amos remarked out loud as he passed papers to Swift. "Perhaps there were times when he chose to believe what he wanted to believe."

It was fascinating reading, containing as it did Jones's intermittent notes to himself detailing his increasing doubts about the business. He had become almost paranoid about the case.

Sure enough, the last comment indicated his intention to get Joanna Stevens to check the books – and the right set of books at that. It had become clear as Amos progressed through the file that Jones felt Warren was not above keeping a set of bogus accounts to satisfy his creditor's growing suspicions.

Chapter 8

Amos carefully put the papers back into the file and rose from his chair.

"I wasn't planning to talk immediately to this woman Scott Warren claimed to be with on Saturday night," he told Swift, "but let's see how far she corroborates his story. No doubt he's warned her but it can't be helped. We might be able to catch her out if she's just covering for him.

"And while we're at it, let's see if Warren said anything to her about Ray Jones's love life.

"I think we can leave Warren to stew a bit. If he is our killer I don't think anyone else is in danger while he knows we're checking up on him."

It was a few miles down quiet country roads to the village where Scott Warren had said his Saturday night date lived. The house itself looked very expensive, detached with a wide frontage and a double garage.

Amos knocked loudly on the large brass knocker on the front door. There was no sound of movement from inside but Swift remarked: "I'm sure I can hear voices. Is that a television or radio?"

The inspector knocked again a little louder. There was still no response. Swift opened the letterbox to listen.

"There's definitely a TV on," she said. "And there's definitely someone in the house because they've turned the sound up."

Swift wandered along the front of the house. As she approached the window at the far end she could see the flickering light of the TV. A woman in her mid to late 20s was sitting in silk pyjamas and a silk dressing gown watching it.

The detective sergeant tapped on the window. The woman looked up, weighed up Swift then slowly and reluctantly prised herself out of the chair and came to the front door, where she was surprised to find not one but two strangers.

Amos already had his warrant card out and poked it in front of her eyes.

"Miss Olivia Spelling?" he asked and, when the woman nodded, added sarcastically: "Sorry to disturb you. Did we wake you?"

Sarcasm seemed to be wasted on her, however, and she merely grunted.

"I thought it was Scott coming to grovel," she said.

"So I take it Mr Warren rang you this morning to warn you we'd be coming," Amos said as he pushed unceremoniously into the house before Spelling could object. He could see no other explanation for why she would assume that the police officers knew who Scott was.

"Oh, he's rung all right but I haven't answered. I wouldn't give him the pleasure. He can come round and grovel and then he can clear off. I'm finished with him."

"How do you know it was him ringing if you didn't answer?" Swift asked. "You thought it was him at the door but it wasn't."

Spelling looked quite baffled. They were now in the room with the television. She turned down the volume but did not switch it off, which Swift found irritating.

Amos just ignored it and asked: "When did you last see Mr Warren?"

He offered no explanation for his question, nor did Spelling seek one.

"Saturday night, of course. He needn't have bothered. He was in a funny mood from the start. Scott used to be such fun. Now he's middle aged and boring."

Swift perked up at the mention of Warren being in a funny mood the day after Ray Jones was presumably murdered but Amos wanted to hear about Warren as a person before getting to the nitty gritty.

It was curious, he thought, that Olivia Spelling hadn't asked why they were there. If she had not answered the phone that day and had not, from the look of her attire, been out, then she probably hadn't heard of Ray Jones's death – unless Warren was indeed the murderer and had confessed to her on Saturday night. That would at least account for why the evening had gone so badly.

"He didn't look that old to me," Amos ventured.

"Well he wouldn't to you, would he, I mean," Spelling countered. "No offence meant, but you're not exactly a spring chicken either, are you?"

Amos nodded and Swift stifled a giggle.

"It was great when I first knew him," Spelling went on. "All clubs and parties. He even took me to London and we went to some great night spots – you know, the ones where the young royals go. His friends knew how to splash the champagne around.

"Now he's SO boring. He never wants to go anywhere expensive. And do you know what he said on Saturday?"

Spelling waited for an answer.

Receiving none, she told them: "He called me flighty and vacuous. Me? Whatever vacuous means."

Amos leaned forward, preferring to step in with one of his own questions rather than pick through the minefield of answering the one put to him.

"Was it a bit sudden, Mr Warren getting middle aged?" he asked.

"No, well, yes, sort of," Spelling replied unhelpfully. "It's sort of been coming for a while but it's just got a lot worse. He didn't want to go out at all on Saturday."

"Did he give a reason?"

"Said he was a bit stuck for cash. Stuck for cash? I ask you."

"Did you ever meet Mr Warren's neighbour, Ray Jones? Did he ever say anything about him?"

"No, I don't think so. Name doesn't ring a bell."

"Please think very carefully before you answer this next question," Amos said slowly and deliberately. "Did Mr Warren mention Mr Jones on Saturday night?"

"No, I told you. I've never heard of him."

"Thank you very much, Miss Spelling." Amos said, rising. "We appreciate your help."

As they walked from the front door to the car, Swift commented: "She never once asked why we were there. Vacuous or what?"

Chapter 9

Amos and Swift returned to Horncastle police station where an incident room had now been set up.

Realistically, given that there was no sign of a forced entry, there seemed to be two possibilities: that Scott Warren had indeed made the dangerous but possible leap across the gap between his laundry and that of Jones, or Jones had been murdered by a lover.

In the latter case there were again two possibilities: Jones had let his lover in or the woman in question had a key.

There was little to point in any specific direction but the one person who might provide the answer was Sarah Miles. Amos and Swift agreed that they should next pursue her properly.

Miles had recovered much of her composure by the time they arrived at her modest home. She reminded Amos of a small timid creature. She seemed to have gathered comforting bits and pieces around her like a hamster in its cage. Odd pages of newspaper littered a coffee table and the floor around her chair. Most pages contained news items of a religious nature or features on serious music. Amos expected her at any minute to start chewing them up and building a nest in a corner.

She eyed Amos and Swift coldly and with suspicion as they sat facing each other, cup and saucer in hand.

"You left four messages on Mr Jones's answering machine," Amos said to her. "Why was that?" he asked simply.

"Why do you think?" Miles retorted. "Raymond never missed Sunday evensong. Not without telling me. I'd spoken to him only on Friday and he said he would be there."

"But you were not sufficiently concerned to go round to his flat to see if his car was there and if he was all right?"

"Don't point the finger at me," Miles came back with surprising vehemence. "The vicar wouldn't listen. Raymond's own office wasn't bothered. His housekeeper wouldn't put herself out. I rang the police and no one took any notice. If you had done your duty and gone round to his flat you might have saved him."

A sob interrupted Miles's flow.

"No one could have saved him," Amos interrupted. "We are satisfied that he died on Friday night, Saturday at the latest.

"But let's get back to your actions. Why didn't you go to his flat on the Monday, then?"

"I went to his office and they hadn't seen him. They wouldn't take matters seriously, either. And that useless housekeeper of his who didn't look after him properly wouldn't stir herself. No one cared about Raymond except me."

Having defended herself with a little more spirit than Amos expected, she was creeping forlornly into her corner.

"So you didn't have a key, then?"

"What are you implying?" Miles's angry, defensive tone was edging back.

"I'm implying that as a friend you might have had a key," Amos said quietly.

"Well I didn't," Miles snapped. "Who Raymond gave a key to his own home was entirely up to him."

Others whom Amos had thought would be angry accepted the circumstances and the questioning better than he had expected; Miles had a sharp tongue that belied her mousy nature.

"I simply find it hard to understand, Miss Miles, why you raised the issue with the vicar, the police, with Mr Jones's office and with his housekeeper – even with his answering machine – and yet you did not take the simple precaution of checking if his car was at Killiney Court or of going up to his flat and knocking on the front door."

"I didn't see why I should go chasing after him," Miles said truculently. "He told me he would be away on Sunday afternoon but that he would be back in time for evensong. I don't have a key to his flat."

Amos was slightly flummoxed by these non-sequiturs that did not answer his question. It appeared that Miles did not intend to account willingly for her lack of action.

"Did you know where he was going on Sunday afternoon?"

"He didn't tell me. I asked him but he wouldn't say. He was hiding something. He couldn't bring himself to tell me. Anyway, it was none of my business."

I'm sure you wanted to make it your business, Amos thought to himself.

"Whoever he saw," Miles went on, "she's got something to account for" and, as Amos raised his eyebrows, "or him," she added hastily.

"Do you know where his wife is?" Amos asked.

Miles looked startled and a reddened a little. She could not meet Amos's eyes.

"How should I know where his wife is? I haven't seen her since she left him. I don't know why he didn't just divorce her and get on with a new life. It was years ago."

"You were close to Mr Jones?" Amos asked. "Close ... friends?" He hesitated deliberately between the two words. Miles went slightly redder and stared down at the floor.

"Mr Jones was a fine man. Everybody liked him. He was a staunch supporter of the church – and he stood by his friends."

Amos noted that after the personal question Raymond had suddenly become Mr Jones. Miles managed to look up briefly.

"Forgive me, Miss Miles," Amos said gently, "but in my experience no-one is universally liked. Surely Mr Jones would make enemies in his business dealings. It would be virtually impossible to do otherwise. Do you know of anyone who would bear a grudge against him?"

"Certainly not. No-one would want to kill Mr Jones. They must have got the wrong person. And no-one," she stressed, "would kill Raymond."

"Was he popular among the other churchgoers?" Swift interceded.

Miles looked at her with some scorn.

"Church is not a popularity poll," she said disdainfully. "You go to church to worship and praise your maker, not to score points with your fellow human beings. Raymond was a good Christian who respected and helped his fellow men and women," she went on proudly. "It was a privilege to know him."

"Did you see much of Mr Jones outside the church?"

"Not particularly," Miles snapped. She shuffled her feet uneasily. "I saw him occasionally in town, just like a lot of other people. Churchgoers have to shop, you know. We have to buy our loaves and fishes."

"And you saw Mr Jones on the Friday afternoon before he died?"

"You seem to know an awful lot," Miles commented, forgetting that she had herself referred indirectly to the meeting. "I saw him briefly in the market square. We exchanged a few words, that's all."

"And was that the last time you saw him?" Amos inquired. "Before you went to his flat this morning."

"Yes," Miles managed after a slight pause. There was again the trace of a sob in her voice. Her eyes, which had finally managed to meet his again, looked back to the floor but Amos could see genuine tears brimming. He did not fancy a stint as comforter.

"That's all for now, Miss Miles," he said in a kindly voice. "We'll show ourselves out."

"I can't feel we've got any further forward," Swift remarked as they walked to their car. "She was just plain evasive when it came to things that mattered."

"Yes," Amos replied thoughtfully.

Chapter 10

Amos and Swift returned to Killiney Court where they had left a team of police officers taking statements from all available residents.

Constable Martin, he of the deft touch with the computer, was waiting excitedly.

"I think you should hear what the Browns have to say, Sir," he informed Amos.

The inspector raised an eyebrow.

"Potential murderers?" he inquired with a touch of humour in his voice.

"Oh no, Sir," Martin added hastily. "They're a harmless old couple who wouldn't hurt a fly. In any case, they've had no dealings with Jones. They hardly ever spoke to him."

"How intriguing," remarked Amos. "What could they possibly have to say?"

Fred and May Brown lived in flat 6D. It was furnished tastefully and adequately but not ostentatiously. May Brown indicated a comfortable arm chair to Amos and took her place on the sofa next to her husband. Swift claimed the other arm chair while the constable took a dining chair.

The Browns were in their 80s but looked 70. The only hint of their real age was the slightly drawn look that came from the back twinges that had prevented Mr Brown, rather than his wife, from coming to the door as the etiquette of those of that age decreed.

"Sorry not to get up, Sir," Mr Brown apologised. "It's a bit difficult once I've got settled."

"I'd like you to tell the detective inspector what you told me," the constable said.

It was Mrs Brown who took up the story: "This young man came to see us about the dreadful business across the way. Naturally we couldn't help much. Mr Brown and I hardly knew Mr Jones even though we lived directly opposite. We spoke, of course, and were on civil terms but no more than that.

"I'm afraid we don't go out much as it's a bit more of an effort these days, what with my knees and Mr Brown's back. We didn't see anyone at all over the weekend."

Despite her protested lack of information, Mrs Brown was in full flood.

"Mr Brown was an auctioneer on market days in three of the towns round about. We were town types ourselves but we bought this place with a bit of countryside around but near enough to Horncastle when Mr Brown retired and sold the business. We went into the town for the formation dancing and the bridge club. But we don't get out as much as we used to.

"I've a touch of arthritis in my knee and Mr Brown's back plays up from all the boxes of agricultural produce he used to hump around on auction days."

Amos shifted in his chair and looking inquiringly at the constable to ask: "What on earth is so fascinating about this couple?"

The young officer looked embarrassed and nipped in quickly before Mrs Brown could launch into further irrelevance.

"Mrs Brown, please tell Inspector Amos about the thefts."

"Oh that," said Mrs Brown, slightly deflated. "But that had nothing to do with Mr Jones. He was far too successful to resort to petty thieving. The amounts involved were never much."

"The amounts of what?" Amos asked, his interest stirred.

"The things that went missing. You know, cash and ornaments and trinkets and the like. We changed our lock and we were all right after that."

Fred Brown cut in: "Let me explain, dear. I'm afraid you've jumped around a bit.

"Inspector, we moved in two years ago with the first batch of residents. We could afford to buy outright with the proceeds of the sale of my business. Then we sold our existing house and invested the money to pay the maintenance charges here and supplement our pensions. We live, as you can see, quite comfortably but not outlandishly."

Amos nodded. Brown had paused to check that the officer wanted him to continue in this vein.

As Mrs Brown made to fill the gap, Amos hastily intervened: "Go on, Mr Brown. I'm with you."

Brown picked up his tale: "Within six months the place was full and so far no-one has left. Well, it's early days yet. Anyway, almost from the start we suspected things were going missing. At first we thought odd items had been mislaid in the move."

He chuckled. "We started teasing each other that we were putting things in the wrong place and then forgetting what we had done with them. We put it down to old age.

"We keep some cash in the top drawer of the sideboard. Sometimes there wasn't as much there as we thought there should be. Again, we each assumed that the other had taken a bit out. But it did seem strange, as we don't go out all that much now and we generally go out together since I retired.

So there was no reason for one of us to take any cash unless we were both there.

"We didn't see a lot of the other flat owners so it was a few weeks before we started to realise that the same thing had happened to other people. One day when we went out Mr Jones and Mr Warren were having a – shall we say heated – discussion in the common area in front of the lifts.

"You've probably seen that each laundry area faces the laundry of a flat opposite. Well, Mr Jones accused Mr Warren of getting across into his laundry and removing some antique porcelain. He collected it, you see – in fact he started at one of my auctions.

"Mr Warren said Mr Jones had so many pieces that he didn't know where he had put them.

"Mr Jones said Mr Warren had some planks stacked in his laundry area and could easily have laid them across the gap and climbed over. Mr Warren was redecorating his flat right through and said the people who worked for the property company had no taste. The planks belonged to the decorators.

"Mr Jones was right about that because we saw the men carrying in trestles and planks to stand on to reach the ceilings more easily. The whole thing would have been quite farcical if it hadn't been so bitter. Still, we started asking round and several other residents said bits and pieces had gone missing.

"We put a note through all the other doors in the block inviting people who had lost things to a meeting in our flat. About half of the residents turned up. It was a bit of a crush getting them all in. We never expected so many to come.

"By this stage we had been in over a year and everyone else at least six months. I'm afraid, though, we simply caused a lot of ill feeling. Accusations flew round the room, some residents stopped talking to each other and the whole meeting broke up in chaos. Nothing was decided.

"Next day Mrs Brown and I counted out some money and left it in the top drawer: a five pound note, six pounds and 65p in small change. We made a point of going out every day for about an hour as long as my back could stand it.

"Each time we came back we counted the cash and it was all there. We had just started to believe that we had imagined the whole thing when on the fifth occasion some of the money had gone. The £5 note was still there but two pounds, half the silver and half the copper had vanished. Whoever had taken it clearly hoped we wouldn't notice.

"Next day I went out alone while Mrs Brown stayed on guard. I bought a lock and replaced the one on the front door. Nothing ever went missing again, though we have left a carefully counted amount of cash in the drawer ever since just in case."

Mr Brown nodded to his wife who got up, went over to the sideboard and pulled the drawer right out. She carried it over to Amos to show him.

"Did you ever report this to the police?" asked Amos, although he knew what the answer would be.

Mr Brown looked embarrassed.

"No, we didn't," Mrs Brown said firmly. "The amounts were quite small and we didn't think you would take it seriously. We were just a couple of old fogies who got flustered."

It was the turn of Amos to look embarrassed. The woman was quite right. Here were two pensioners who had to protect themselves against petty crime.

"And did you have any idea who had gained access to your flat?" Amos inquired. "Presumably you are vulnerable through the laundry area as well?"

"Oh no," burst in Mrs Brown with a laugh. "Old Mrs Atkinson could never get across there."

She hesitated.

"My wife and I discussed this matter after talking to the constable," said Brown. "We knew you were likely to ask at some point. We don't feel it is right to point the finger when we have not a shred of evidence against anyone."

"This is a murder inquiry," Amos said quietly. "I think you had better tell me."

Mrs Brown, despite the twinges of her conscience, was patently quite eager to speak out now she had the officer's blessing.

"Two people were here when these flats were council owned. One was Miss Norman in 5A. She moved out during the renovations then came back into her old flat overlooking the front drive.

"The other was Nick, the caretaker. He occupied the little caretaker's flat on the mezzanine floor. He didn't have to move because they hardly did any work on his place. He kept his job as caretaker because no one got round to sacking him. I suppose they didn't have the heart to get rid of him. He was getting on and they didn't pay him much.

"Anyway," she continued quickly as she caught the exasperated look in Amos's eye, "we think one or the other of them somehow got hold of a set of keys for the entire block. We're not sure if the front doors were changed."

Her husband added: "Naturally we would never have suspected Miss Norman but she does sit at her window overlooking the front drive such a lot. She pretends to be knitting but it looks like the same piece of garment all the time. She can see everyone come and go and she would know which flats were empty.

"In fact, one of the things that came out during our get-together with the rest of the block – as accusations started flying round – was that the whole floor had probably been out when each break-in occurred. It was bound to happen from time to time with only four flats on each floor. Miss Norman would have known when the coast was clear."

"Of course," his wife added as if her conscience troubled her over accusing a neighbour, "Nick would also know who was in or out."

"Did either of them come to the meeting?" Swift interposed.

"Miss Norman did," replied Mr Brown. "But she didn't say anything."

"The poor woman couldn't get a word in," Mrs Brown explained.

"Nick wanted to come," she added suddenly, "but he's not a resident – not a proper resident, anyway. He was quite put out when I said no. He accused me of being a snob."

Swift stifled a giggle a trifle noisily, causing Mrs Brown to glance at her inquisitively.

Even Amos was provoked to smile but he overcame the weakness quickly and started to rise.

"Thank you Mrs Brown ... Mr Brown," he remarked graciously. "You have been very helpful. I hope I shall not need to trouble you again but if I do I am sure I can count on your cooperation."

"Of course," replied Mr Brown. "We quite understand. Please don't hesitate to ask if we can help in any way."

Amos was deep in thought as the three police officers took their leave.

Chapter 11

Amos had not the slightest objection to seeing Jones's body in the mortuary early next day, even though he knew it had been chopped up and sewn back together again. The mortuary was the proper place for a victim of violent death, not the poor fellow's own bedroom. There could be no objection to something, however unpleasant, being in its proper place.

Slater looked up from the cold slab as Amos entered the room. The pathologist was in a better mood. He tended to swing for no particular reason that Amos could divine. Today was a good day.

"Morning," Slater called out cheerfully. "Now let's see what I can tell you.

"Male, fifties. Killed by several blows to the head. Crushed the skull. Didn't stand a chance. Look at the mess," he added, turning over their head to show the left-hand side where the damage had been done.

"Not a pretty sight. Death instantaneous. The first blow would have been enough. No need to bother with the rest – and there were at least five more direct hits plus several smacks scattered round the body. Look at the bruising.

"You'll be pleased to know there's no doubt about the weapon. That iron bar left conveniently by the side of the bed fits the bill nicely. The blows were delivered by just that sort of implement and blood and hair on the bar match Jones perfectly. So at least you don't have to go around looking for a weapon."

"Time of death?" Amos asked.

"Some time Friday night."

"You couldn't narrow it down a bit?" Amos asked hopefully.

"Correct," came the reply. "I couldn't."

Then Slater added as Amos was about to open his mouth: "For heaven's sake, it was Tuesday before I got a go at the body. The longer after the deed was done, the harder it is to be precise about the time."

Seeing the disappointment in Amos's face, Slater relented. "I can help a bit on that, though. From the contents of his stomach I assume he died somewhere around midnight.

"He'd eaten, I should say, about three hours before he was killed. He seems to have had a fair amount of Scotch as a nightcap – not enough to make him drunk but probably enough to make him sleepy. The chances are that he wouldn't have heard an intruder."

There was no point in arguing, so Amos said simply: "Anything else?"

"One or two health matters," Slater volunteered. "Our friend Jones hit the bottle a bit. Not excessively, but his liver was rather enlarged. Also, he was developing a stomach ulcer. Again, nothing serious yet but storing up trouble for later.

"Well, he would have been if someone hadn't cut him short," Slater commented with a hearty laugh.

Amos remained stony faced.

"Rather more serious," the pathologist picked up the thread, "he had had a couple of heart attacks, one major, one minor. If he was still wheeling and dealing he was pushing his luck."

Amos was slightly alarmed. "He did die from the blows to the head?" the officer asked. "I don't want some smarty pants QC getting his client off on a technicality."

"Fear not," came the response. "The heart attacks were history. Heads it is."

Slater laughed heartily again. This was certainly a good day.

"How hard were the blows?" Amos inquired.

"A pretty fair smack," the pathologist replied. "It looks like a quick concentration of blows with one, presumably the last, heavier than the others. Whoever it was meant to be sure Jones was dead."

"Would it have had to be a strong person?"

"Not in the least," Slater responded without hesitation. "That pipe was quite solid. You could get a decent swing with it."

"Thanks," said Amos. "You can put him away again now."

Chapter 12

Murder inquests are hardly worth the bother, Amos remarked to Swift as they made their way out of the back of the police headquarters to their waiting car.

"Would it be impertinent, Sir, to ask, then, why you are so keen to go? It's only the opening. There'll be identification and cause of death, which we already know, and the whole thing will take three minutes maximum from opening to adjournment.

"We won't even get 'murder by person or persons unknown' at this stage in the proceedings."

"We are going, Sgt Swift," Amos replied with good humour, "because murder inquests, predictable though they are, have their own fatal fascination. I can never resist toddling along just to see if anyone unexpected turns up."

This particular occasion would, however, have been one of life's little disappointments had a court official not pointed out the lone figure sitting in one corner as Simon Renshaw.

"He's Jones's solicitor," the official disclosed confidentially.

The only other people present, apart from the coroner, were Sarah Miles, who gave evidence of identification, and the pathologist. The case was adjourned sine die.

Amos introduced himself to the solicitor immediately. Renshaw, balding and greying, was nearing retirement age. His generally sedentary, well fed and wined life had inexorably added inches to his waistline.

But if he had lost his figure and his youth, he had not surrendered his dress code. He wore an immaculate, well fitting pin stripe suit and he was picking his black bowler hat and rolled umbrella from the stand by the door as Amos approached him.

"I have to say, Inspector," he replied to Amos's request for a few minutes of his time, "I don't greatly like discussing a client's private legal business with third parties, not even the police, but in view of the circumstances I'm prepared to help as far as professional etiquette allows.

"My office is just two minutes' walk across the market square. I had set aside half an hour in case the hearing ran over unexpectedly."

The office had the same old-fashioned, reassuring air of its owner, with leather furniture and leather-bound books. Renshaw, of Renshaw, Renshaw and Ogylvie, had given up the quill and ink pot of his father but had declined to progress as far as a ball point pen.

He laid his fountain pen on the desk in front of him ceremoniously.

"I appreciate your concerns," Amos finally broke the silence, "but I do need to know who benefits in Mr Jones's will."

Renshaw did not even have to get out the document.

"Mr Jones made only two wills in his lifetime. The first was a few years after his marriage. He should have made one straight away but like the rest of us he did not wish to admit that he would ever die.

"In that will he left everything to his wife. He made his second will a year ago."

Amos was immediately aroused.

"Did he make many changes?" he asked.

"Not a great deal," came the response. "His wife remained the residual beneficiary but he made a few minor bequests. These were for Sarah Miles, a friend; a chap called Jim Berry who helped him a great deal with his business; and finally the church he had taken to attending in his later years."

"Large amounts?"

"Just a few thousand pounds in total. Mrs Jones was still very well provided for."

"Was Mr Jones content with this arrangement? Are you aware of any plans he might have had to change the will again?"

Renshaw hesitated.

"I'd be obliged, inspector, if this conversation could be kept confidential between ourselves. Mr Jones had indicated to me that he intended to reduce the bequest to Miss Miles but he had not yet settled on a figure. I had the impression that he did not intend to cut her out altogether but it was, after all, the largest of the three bequests."

Amos subsided. The will offered no real motive for murdering Jones at this particular juncture. People had admittedly killed for relatively small amounts and it was just possible that Miles had discovered that her legacy was to be reduced but it seemed rather tenuous.

"How well did you know Raymond Jones?" Amos tried a different tack.

Renshaw was ill at ease. He did not regard discussing Jones on a personal level as a breach of professional confidence yet it seemed, if anything, worse, somehow disrespectful.

"I'm sorry to ask," Amos assured him on seeing his discomfort, "but I must tell you quite frankly that we have a very wide field of possible suspects and nothing that points to any particular individual. Anything that might help us to narrow the scope of the inquiry could set us a long way forward in bringing Mr Jones's killer to justice. I need hardly remind you that this was a particularly merciless attack."

These words had the desired effect of assuaging Renshaw's conscience.

"My father knew Raymond Jones senior. He ran a general stores in the town – groceries, hardware and so on. He set up before the second world war and kept going through the 40s and 50s.

"Jones senior had two sons and a daughter. The girl worked hard in the shop and kept it going when her father's health began to fail. The two boys showed no such enthusiasm. Neither wanted to put the effort into a business whose days, they felt, were numbered."

Renshaw sighed.

"In a way, I suppose they were right," he went on. "Supermarkets were just starting to come in and the writing was on the wall for traditional retailers. Old Mr Jones couldn't or wouldn't see it and his daughter didn't know how to contradict him.

"The chap was heartbroken that his sons didn't want to follow him into the business and he was of that generation of fathers who thought girls didn't count in business. They would go off and get married and have children. He died of cancer in his early 50s, leaving the business, quite unjustly, to the two sons who didn't want it and leaving his own daughter virtually destitute.

"She married a childhood sweetheart who still carried a torch for her, though I think her enthusiasm for the match had waned somewhat over the years. She certainly felt bitter about the whole business but there was nothing I could do for her.

"My father had drawn up the will and it was watertight. He, like Mr Jones senior, believed girls found husbands who would look after them so he did nothing to persuade his client to make proper provision for her. She left the area a couple of years later and I have no idea where she is now.

"The two boys promptly sold the business and split the proceeds. That was how Raymond Jones got started. He certainly demonstrated a good head for business. He got quite an inflated price from a supermarket keen to expand into the area.

"You may hear rumours," the solicitor added quite unnecessarily, "that Raymond Jones cheated his brother Leonard on the deal. I can assure you that such suggestions are utterly without foundation. My father acted in the sale of the business.

"Leonard, like his sister, subsequently left Lincolnshire while Raymond set up as a builder's merchant. He saw there was money in building. He diversified into plant hire and construction and sold a thriving business to a medium-sized conglomerate anxious to build up nationwide coverage. He invested the money in more businesses and even bought back part of his construction company a few years later for a pittance. He was a shrewd operator.

"I took over as his solicitor from my father about halfway through his career."

"If Mr Jones was so successful in his business deals he must have engendered a fair amount of envy," Amos commented.

"Mr Jones made friends and foes. He was a very generous employer. He inspired great loyalty in his staff. That was one of the reasons why he was so successful. However, I concede that you can't be in business for that length of time without rubbing some people up the wrong way. Yes, there were those who were jealous. Some of the people he got the better of no doubt resented the fact."

"Do you, or did you, also act for Mrs Jones?"

"I acted for Mr and Mrs Jones when they bought their marital home. Otherwise no. I don't think she's ever had much need of a solicitor. Like father, like son, Raymond Jones believed in male and female territory. He wasn't quite as old-fashioned in that respect as his father. It was though, only at my firm suggestion that the house was bought in joint names purely because it made sense if Mr Jones died first."

Amos was thoughtful.

He said: "In the event, the couple split up. The house was presumably sold and the proceeds divided. Did you arrange all that?"

Renshaw looked slightly peeved.

"I did the paperwork for the sale of the house, yes, so technically I acted for Mrs Jones then as well. But all the arrangements were made by Mr Jones and the money from the sale went straight into his bank account. I was very unhappy about it but Mrs Jones concurred in the arrangement so I thought of it as acting purely for Mr Jones rather than for them as a couple."

And did she concur willingly, Amos wondered.

One final question: "Do you know where Mrs Jones is now?"

"I haven't the faintest idea."

Chapter 13

Amos had decided from the outset that he would interview the caretaker himself and the routine statement taken along with those of all the residents in the block was so unhelpful that he doubled his resolve.

Here was a man who saw all the comings and goings. Admittedly, the security guards did, too, but they worked shifts while Nick Foster was bustling around all the time. Besides, Foster had been on the scene a long time and was likely to know the tenants better. The guards could wait their turn, although Amos was certainly going to talk to those who had been on duty that fateful weekend.

Foster was not, however, sweeping leaves when the detective inspector and Swift came looking for him. Amos found him skulking around in his cubby hole of a residence on the mezzanine floor. Foster was a while answering the solid knock on his shabby door – refurbishment was for wealthy tenants like Ray Jones, not impoverished old caretakers like Nick Foster.

The door eventually opened three or four inches. Foster was unable to conceal his considerable nervousness.

"Yes?" he uttered hoarsely.

"Police," replied Amos clearly. He produced his warrant card. Foster open the door another couple of inches and stood waiting, his eyes fixed intently on his visitor's face.

"It would be a lot easier if I could come in," Amos suggested pleasantly.

"There's not much room," Foster said sheepishly. "I haven't got much space for myself."

Nonetheless, Amos met with no resistance as he pushed open the reluctant door.

Foster was not lying about the lack of space. Bric-a-brac of all descriptions cluttered the small room, some in boxes, some scattered around the floor. There were ornaments, glassware, a wig on a chair. Foster appeared to be a man of catholic tastes.

"You've quite a collection," Amos observed.

Foster looked shifty. "Just a bit of stuff people have given me over the years. No, not there," he added hastily as Amos made to sit down on a packing case. "The top's a bit wonky. Don't want you falling in and breaking anything."

"Or hurting myself," Amos remarked dryly. "You live here alone?"

"Yes, I've been on my own since my wife died 30 odd years ago. Cancer. They couldn't do much about it in those days."

"Did you come here when the flats reopened after the refurbishment?"

Foster snorted. "I've been here a lot longer than that. I was caretaker in the old days when it was owned by the council. They always treated me fair, they did. Not like this lot."

"You resent the influx of wealthier people, perhaps?"

"That's nothing to do with it. I was stuck in here while all the building dust was flying around. And did they do anything for me? Not likely! I'm still stuck in this cubbyhole of a place with not a penn'rth of work done on it."

"And do you resent the people here?" Amos persisted. "Did you resent Ray Jones?"

"You're not pinning that on me," exclaimed Foster indignantly, half rising. "I get blamed for everything else around here. I'm not being blamed for murder."

"Did you know Ray Jones? What was he like?" Amos persisted, ignoring Foster's protestations.

"Jones was all right, I suppose," Foster continued grumpily. "He was all right with me, anyway. Always civil. But I didn't know him properly," Foster was quick to add.

"Did he get on well with the other residents?"

"Some he did, some he didn't. He had a right old barney with that Scott Warren who lives next door to him. I told you about that right after you found the body.

"He was on bad terms with the Smiths on the top floor. Jack Smith hated his guts. Ray Jones did the dirty on him over a business deal and pinched one of his best clients. Mr Smith nearly went bust.

"But he managed to pull his business out of the fire and made good. He was spitting blood when he found out Mr Jones was moving in to the same block of flats but he'd already put a deposit down and the developers wouldn't let him have his money back. Finally they let him switch to a top floor flat so he could be as far away from Jones as possible," Foster chuckled.

"They were going to be next door to each other. Smith had to pay extra for the top floor because it's got a better view. He wasn't too pleased about that, either."

Foster chuckled again. "I think that annoyed him more than the business deal."

"What was the deal they fell out over?" Swift asked.

"I have no idea," Foster returned. "Why don't you ask Jack Smith? I'll tell you this, though. They didn't speak to each other if they met."

Foster chuckled again.

"One day I saw them come down in the lift together. Ray Jones must have got in when Smith was on the way down. Jones came out smirking and Smith's face was as black as thunder.

"He held back until Jones was well clear. It didn't matter so much to Jones. He'd got the better of the deal. I know for a fact that Smith threatened he would get his revenge but he never did.

"Mind you, Mrs Smith took it worse. She felt her husband had been humiliated. You want to ask her."

"Let's get back to the Friday night," Amos interposed. "What did you do after seeing Mr Jones and Mr Scott having a disagreement?"

"Yes, that's right!" Foster exclaimed eagerly. "A right dingdong. He's another you should talk to. I told you so last time."

"Your movements on Friday night," Amos prompted wearily.

"I was sweeping up. It took ages. Not that anyone appreciates it," Foster grumbled. "There was dust everywhere. They were finishing off putting the barrier in. And that silly hut they got from outside Buckingham Palace. Dust everywhere. It was a good job it didn't rain. You can imagine the mess that would have made.

"Anyway," he added hastily as he sensed that Amos's patience was wearing thin. "Anyway, I cleaned up until about nine o'clock. It was quite warm ... like I say, at least it wasn't raining.

"Then I came back here and watched telly for an hour and went to bed. Well, they don't pay me to work all night," he added defensively. "They don't even pay me to work till nine."

"What did you watch?" Swift asked sweetly.

Foster replied without hesitation. *"Have I Got News for You.* You know, that quiz programme about the papers and where they're all rude to each other. I like that. Then there was *Never Mind the Buzzards* or something like that. It's about pop music but I don't understand half of it. I don't even know what the name of the programme is supposed to mean. I got a bit fed up of it so I turned it off and went to bed. I was tired out. I'd been working all day."

"Did you hear anything during the night?" Swift asked.

"Nothing at all," Foster replied rather too eagerly. "I told you, I was tired out. Slept like a log. Well, I'm not the night watchman," he added with a little unnecessary aggression. "It's not my job to check who comes and goes. I wasn't the one deserting my post."

"What do you mean?" Amos asked sharply.

"That night watchman who was on duty on Friday night. That's who I mean. Always nipping around the back for a fag. They're not supposed to smoke on duty, you know. That's why he got me to watch out for him all afternoon."

"Surely he wouldn't still have been here late at night if he was on duty during the day," Swift ventured.

"Course he was," Foster retorted with a note of contempt. "They don't pay 'em much. That's because they're all thick. They only have to sit there and press a button. They employ anyone. Imbeciles, criminals ... and pay peanuts. They don't run any proper checks on who they employ. So the guards work double shifts to bump up their wages. The same chap who came in at noon was there till midnight. At least, that's what he told me.

"So who manned the gate when he went for a ciggie after nine o'clock?"

Foster triumphantly left the question hanging in the air.

Swift shot Amos a glance but he deliberately ignored her look.

"Thank you, Mr Foster," he said calmly. "You have been most helpful. We know where to find you if we need you again."

"Can't see why you should," Foster replied truculently. "I've already given you your two top suspects."

"I'll be the judge of that," Amos responded coldly. "But thank you for your cooperation, anyway."

Foster was clearly not sorry to see them go. Once they were out on the landing with the caretaker's door closed behind them, Swift turned to Amos.

"You realise if what he says is true anyone could have walked in and murdered Jones," she said. "It doesn't have to have been one of the residents or someone he brought in."

"The point had crossed my mind," Amos said dejectedly.

Chapter 14

Amos sauntered casually up to the sentry box as the guard watched him with a cautious eye.

Neither spoke until the officer was at the door of the little hut.

"You were on duty on Friday night," Amos said more as a statement than a question.

"Yes." The reply was perfunctory.

This is going to be heavy going, Amos thought, but at least he had the guard trapped inside the box.

"Did anyone come in that evening who was not a resident?"

The guard took out a red covered book.

"All visitors are recorded here," he said, opening the book at the relevant page.

Amos could see just three entries. A young lady had visited 7B, arriving at 7pm and leaving next morning, collaborating the story of the young man in that flat, who told the officer who interviewed him that the woman had been in his flat all night.

A couple had called for 9C about a quarter of an hour later. They were booked out at 11 pm. This, too, fitted in with the statement given by the residents of the relevant apartment.

No-one else in Killiney Court had admitted to having outside company that evening. Yet one person was shown to have signed in at 9pm on Friday evening without any record of his or her departure, either that night or subsequently. Amos sighed. The record keeping was so haphazard it was pointless.

Amos scrutinised the childlike scrawl that passed for a signature.

"Joan … Jean … John," Swift ventured over his shoulder.

The surname was illegible but the box demanding the visitor's name in block letters offered more scope, though the contents were equally poorly written.

"It couldn't be John," ventured the nightwatchman. "I remember. It was a woman."

"Joan Thornton, then," Amos decreed. "That second letter isn't an E. Did you see her leave?"

"No, no," the sentry replied a little too eagerly. "She must have stayed the night and left after the next guy came on duty. I can't tell you who it was. You'll have to ask him."

"Well, at least we can decipher the flat she visited," Swift offered in consolation. "That must be 5C. I know the 5 looks more like an S but it can't be any other number and that letter is definitely C."

Swift looked round. She spotted her friend from uniformed branch, Jane Wyman, she of the film star name and film star looks, keeping guard near the lift, and called her over.

"Jane, she said, "Weren't you assigned to level 5? Do you by any chance remember who lives in 5C?"

"I remember the woman," PC Wyman responded after a moment's pause. "I could hardly forget her. She was very tubby tummed – late stages of pregnancy," she translated quickly as she caught Amos's enquiring eye.

"She was so far gone I was afraid the shock of being interviewed in a murder inquiry would send her into labour. I remember she particularly said that no-one ever visited her."

"Midwife?" Amos asked. "The baby's father?"

"No-one," said Swift flatly. "She was quite definite."

"These people walked in?" Amos turned back to the keeper of the gate.

"Visitors have to use the two bays outside the barrier to park," the guard responded. "We're instructed not to let them drive in. All the bays inside are allocated, one to each flat."

"Supposing one of the residents drives in with a passenger. Do they have to be logged in?"

"No."

"So non-residents can get access to the block without being recorded?" Amos persisted.

"Don't blame me," the guard retorted. "I don't make the rules. We're only told to take the names of unaccompanied visitors. Residents who bring guests in with them are expected to take responsibility for them. You can't keep a check on everybody."

"In fact," said Amos suddenly, "you can't even account for everyone who comes in on foot, can you?"

"It's all here in the book," the guard answered defensively, "like I told you."

He was studying the officer's features closely, trying to work out what Amos knew.

The inspector paused for a few seconds.

"You were on duty from noon to midnight?"

"Yes."

"But you weren't at your post all that time, were you?"

"The caretaker just kept an eye open while I nipped to the toilet a couple of times. I was only gone half a minute. Blimey, I have to go to the toilet occasionally," the guard added belligerently.

Amos was unflustered. "It wasn't the toilet I was thinking of," he remarked casually. "How many cigarettes did you smoke in that time?"

The guard was clearly rattled. "Only one or two. Nick kept an eye on things for me. I wasn't gone long.

"Look," he added, "you won't tell the security company will you? They don't have to know. I'd get the sack if they found out. We're not supposed to smoke. Some of the residents don't like it so I make sure no one sees me. You don't have to tell the boss, do you?"

By the end of his outpouring the guard was practically pleading.

"It depends on how far you collaborate," Amos replied coolly. "We could start with the truth about Friday night."

"Look," said the harassed guard, "I did go for a smoke a few times while Nick was around. He kept watch from under the building so he could spot anyone coming and call me. As a matter fact, he did call me out a couple of times but I got back to the barrier in time to check people in.

"Look," he added eagerly, opening the red book again. "Here are the entries for that afternoon. You only asked about the evening so I didn't point them out to you earlier."

Amos was not, in fact, particularly interested in the earlier arrivals, both of whom were recorded leaving before Jones had returned to the block. However, the sentinel's attitude and admission confirmed Foster's revelation that he left his post and disappeared behind the block where he could not see who was coming or going.

"But Foster was not there in the evening, was he?" Amos persisted. "And we've no idea whether this mystery woman – Jean, er Joan, Thornton – left that night or not?"

The wretched guard looked around like a frightened, cornered rat. Amos gave him a bolthole.

"I shall not report this matter to your employers unless I have to. But I must know how many times you left this post unattended and for how long. If you don't co-operate I have no choice but to talk to the firm. I hope you can see that."

"Three times for about five minutes. No more."

Think of a number and double it, Amos advised himself. He probably left the gate half a dozen times for up to 10 minutes at a stretch.

"The barrier was down all the time," the guard added sullenly. "No one drove in or out."

"It doesn't take much to duck under the bar and walk in, though, does it?" Amos retorted. "We can just about rule out the elderly and the arthritic," he added with heavy sarcasm. "Everyone else is a suspect."

The guard hung his head ashamedly. He made to speak, then thought better of reminding Amos of his promise not report the incident to his boss.

"Well that's it, then," Amos told Swift a few minutes later. "Everybody and his dog is a suspect now. Jones had business dealings with half the county. Where do we start?"

Chapter 15

"I think," Amos told Swift at police HQ just outside Lincoln next morning, "we had better pay another visit to Jones's office. If we have to interview all his business contacts we'd better find out the extent of the bad news."

"Just when we'd worked our way through the Killiney Court residents and thought we were narrowing it down," Swift grumbled. "Shall I get someone to go and get a list?" she asked, hoping to deflect what would patently be a laborious task away from herself.

"That won't be necessary," her boss replied simply. "I want to go down there myself. You'd better come with me."

Swift drove. Traffic was heavy coming into Horncastle for no obvious reason so it was half past nine by the time they arrived. Although it was now well past office opening hours, the nerve centre of Jones's business empire was stricken by lethargy. The lone typist was staring at her recently painted fingernails, leaving the phone to ring in the far corner.

Miss Jade Nolan, Jones's rock upon whom the office stood fast while he was out wheeling and dealing, was drowning in a morass of papers. She was close to tears, patently overcome by genuine grief at the cruel loss of her leader and by the frustrations of enforced inactivity. No one knew who now owned the company, who was in charge, what decisions had to be made nor what to decide anyway.

The office, the empire were in limbo. Nolan seemed almost relieved to see Amos and Swift. Few people in this investigation had been, Amos mused. The office manager stood up, leaving the paper Everest to its fate.

"Inspector Amos," she said with something almost approaching enthusiasm. "I wasn't sure we would see you again. You seemed to lose interest last time you were here, if you'll pardon my saying so."

"Granted," Amos replied. "I doubt if you will welcome my return, though," he continued frankly. "I'm afraid we're going to turn your whole routine upside-down."

Amos did not need to be told that this last remark was ludicrous. The routine had clearly already been sent topsy-turvy. There was nothing to disturb but chaos.

The officer continued briskly: "We shall need a full list of all the people Mr Jones did business with. We shall need details of all the deals he was working on when he died. We also need to know of any companies or individuals that he competed against and anyone who might have held a grudge against him, anyone who lost out to this company."

"I suggest you work in Mr Jones's office," came the response. "I'll take you through."

Once they were in the back room, however, Nolan broke down. Away from the gaze of the office junior, she no longer had to put on a front.

"It isn't fair," she sobbed. "I don't know what to do. I've made sure we get paid for this month but after that what happens? I don't know who to turn to for what happens next."

Then Nolan pulled herself together just as quickly as she had fallen apart.

"I should be ashamed," she said, looking up at Amos instead of at the ground. "Here's me worried about myself when it's poor Mr Jones I should feel sorry for."

"Just take your time, Miss Nolan," Amos said gently. "You've had a very nasty shock and it's quite understandable that you feel responsible for the young woman through there who faces losing her job before she's hardly started it.

"But I suspect that the death of Mr Jones is not just the loss of an employer. I think you had some affection for him."

Nolan stared hard at him, distracted momentarily from her distress.

"I'm astonished," she said, not realising that it was in fact Det Sgt Swift who had realised. "Men never notice these things."

She gave a short, sardonic laugh.

"Ray never noticed," she said, "but then he was still in love with his wife. He didn't really appreciate her until she left him.

"Let's deal with what you came for," she switched suddenly. "Please take care of everything. This was Ray's whole life."

The formal Mr Jones, the employer, had been replaced by Ray, the man who didn't want the women he attracted but had let the woman he did want slip through his fingers.

"All the documents relating to current deals are filed in his desk drawer," Nolan said recovering her composure. "He had a copy of them all and so did I. All of the older deals and documents are in the filing cabinets over there."

Nolan indicated three cabinets, each with four drawers. Amos groaned inwardly.

"I'll have a look through the current files. I'm afraid we will have to take them all away for a thorough search."

"You won't need the older files, will you?" Nolan asked. "Like I say, I've got copies of all the pending deals but not those that have been completed."

"All the files," said Amos firmly. "You surely have it all on computer disks, don't you?"

"Mr Jones wanted it all down on paper. He didn't trust computers in case they crashed and lost all the records."

But she looked away from Amos's steady gaze. She knew he could take what he needed. The office was in too much chaos, the staff too demoralised to mount resistance.

Amos slid open the desk drawers in Jones's room. The one at the bottom had runners for taking files. There were no more than half a dozen. Amos took the three bulkiest ones and handed the rest to Swift.

"What are we looking for?" she asked.

Amos shrugged his shoulders.

"Anything," he replied simply.

Amos studied the first file in his batch. It was Scott Warren's. He read it carefully, despite having scrutinised it on his first visit.

Swift was already closing her third file long before he had finished. She pulled the two unopened files next to Amos's elbow across to her side of the desk and looked up at the higher ranking officer.

He nodded and she opened the first one. Swift had finished the other two files by the time Amos had completed his probe of the Warren dossier.

"I wonder who Jim was," Amos commented as he closed the folder. "Jones seems to have paid someone of that name pocket money to check on how much mail Warren got each day and how often the express couriers called.

"That'll be Jim Berry." Swift responded promptly. "He's in all these files as well. He seems to do all Jones's leg work for him. All the menial jobs and running about. Jones paid him peanuts but he seems to have been a willing worker nevertheless. Anything Jones wanted was always done within a couple of days.

"Jones has written notes on the file every time Berry reported back. Sometimes he is referred to as Berry, sometimes as Jim, occasionally by his full name but it's clearly all the same person. He has a real gift for finding out all sorts of information."

Amos glanced at the entries in turn. On each note a payment was recorded, £5, £10, once £20, all trivial amounts for what was usually a vital piece of information. Jones apparently placed great store by what Jim Berry dug up, for he always acted on the basis of what Berry provided, as witnessed by the final note on each sheet that bore the informant's name.

"Berry must have had a lot of friends in a lot of places," Swift ventured.

Amos thought for a while and the two sat for a couple of minutes in silence. Then the chief inspector rose from his chair, pushed the Warren file across to Swift with the words "Take a look through this for a moment," and sauntered to the door, out into the main office and without asking, made his way to the filing cabinets containing records of deals gone by. Nolan and her assistant watched him with apathy and, in the case of the assistant, mild amusement.

Amos pulled the top drawer. It clanked metal on metal but it would not budge.

"It's locked," Miss Nolan remarked coldly and unnecessarily. "Those are confidential documents."

"The key?" Amos asked, more as a demand than a question.

The head-by-default of the Jones empire produced the required item reluctantly. She unlocked the cabinets.

Amos pulled out the top drawer, keeping his body between it and Nolan to stop her seeing what he was looking at. Nolan sniffed and walked slowly back to her desk. Left to his own devices, Amos glanced along the row of files. Each was clearly labelled, mostly with the name of a company on a Perspex tab.

Amos flicked them forward one by one. The As were sparse but quite a number were deposited among the Bs: Baines & Stokes, Barker and Sons, Bailey Contractors, Beswick George but no Berry, no Berry and something. Amos proceeded methodically through three drawers. Finally, towards the back of the bottom batch, he discovered: Wardle & Berry.

It rang a bell with him. Amos followed the business world very little except when it impinged on his work, but Wardle & Berry had been quite a well known electrical wholesaler in its day. You never heard of it now.

Amos extracted the file and straightened up. Miss Nolan was not pleased and coughed a phoney "ahem" but the officer wandered back into Jones's inner sanctuary and closed the door behind him. Swift was still ploughing through the Warren file but she was getting on faster than Amos had done.

Wardle & Berry was another thick dossier. Amos skimmed through, stopping to study certain pages in greater detail. Soon Swift had finished with Warren and Amos passed selected documents from Wardle & Berry across to her. Swift whistled.

"So Jones destroyed Berry's business," she commented.

"It gets better," Amos returned. "When Jones financed the rival business that drummed Berry's lot out, it looks as if Wardle was in cahoots with Jones. Look at this'" he went on, passing more pages to Swift. "Jones paid Wardle off rather handsomely while Berry ended up with next to nothing.

"In fact," Amos picked up excitedly as he turned more pages in the folder, "Berry went bankrupt and Jones got all the stock and the vans for peanuts. Then he sold them at a profit to the rival wholesaler he was backing. So Jones won twice over, Wardle got out comfortably, and Berry went bust."

"It's enough of a motive for murder," Swift said, reading what Amos was obviously thinking, "but how long ago was this?"

Amos shuffled through the papers again. "About five years ago," he answered.

"So why did he wait so long for his revenge?" Swift posed. "If he was working for Jones he must have had lots of opportunities to settle the score before now. And why wait," she added suddenly as the thought struck her, "until there was a security guard installed outside Jones's home? It doesn't make sense."

"I think it's time we asked Berry himself," Amos said. He ambled to the door and opened it.

"Do you mind if we use the phone?" he called across to Nolan.

"I'm surprised you bother to ask," she replied frostily. "You seem to have helped yourself to everything else."

Amos closed the door and muttered "I'll take that as a yes" to Swift, who giggled. He picked up the handset, rang the office and asked to be put through to Sgt Burke.

"Listen carefully," Amos told the sergeant. "I want three officers down here at Jones's office pronto with a van and cardboard boxes. I shall want a search warrant for the home of a man called Jim Berry ready for me when I get back to the station, plus a team standing by to tear his home apart later this afternoon."

Having relayed the most recent address for Berry given in the files so that the warrant could be applied for, Amos replaced the receiver and went back to the Wardle & Berry file while he awaited the arrival of the three officers. When they duly pulled up outside, he went out to the pavement to greet them.

Amos dropped the filing cabinet key into Sgt Burke's hand. "You stay inside to make sure no-one tries to remove any files behind your backs," Amos instructed him. "The other two load the entire contents of the drawer in Jones's desk and the two filing cabinets in the main office."

As the three arrivals marched in, Amos signalled to Swift to join him outside. They stayed only long enough to see Nolan watch open-mouthed as the ransacking of the precious documents began.

"I think it is also time to take Berry apart," Amos said. "There's someone I want to talk to first, then we'll be ready for Berry."

Chapter 16

"We don't need the car," Amos told Swift. "I took a look at the map on the office wall and the place we want is only five minutes away.

Amos explained his thoughts as he and Swift walked down the narrow lane past Horncastle Parish Church on their right and, on the left, the small premises where William Marwood, the famous hangman who invented the long drop for executions, once had a cobbler's shop.

"According to the files, a woman by the name of Christine Clarkson was working for Jones soon after the incident with Wardle & Berry," Amos said.

"Yes, I noticed the name," Swift replied. "She seems to have been the only employee at the time but I got the impression she wasn't there at the time Jones swindled Berry."

"I think you're right," Amos agreed, "but she has a longer inside knowledge on Jones the businessman stretching back before Nolan. Jones seems to have been quite fond of her. He bought her quite an expensive wedding present when she left to get married and he kept a note of her current address, which is where we're heading now.

"Her married name is Clarke. She gained an 'e' and lost a 'son'."

Christine Clarke lived in a terrace house in Horncastle on the opposite side of the A158 Lincoln to Skegness road. She was not surprised to see the two police officers. Word of Ray Jones's demise had indeed spread quickly.

Her husband was at home, still wearing his postman's uniform, and a toddler was lurching from one item of furniture to the next, frequently falling down in the process but immediately picking herself up and trying again cheerfully.

"How long have you been married?" Amos asked pleasantly.

"Two years," Mrs Clarke said, taking the inquiry at face value as genuine interest.

"I'm two," the little girl announced proudly.

"Not yet, darling," her mother said with a laugh. "Soon."

"You worked for Ray Jones for several years, I believe," Amos said.

"Yes, I joined him straight from school. He knew the headmaster and came in one day and said he was looking for a school leaver to do office work. I was 16 and about to leave school and hadn't any idea what to do. I was a pretty good reader and not bad at maths but my parents couldn't afford to send me to secretarial school. It seemed like a good opportunity and none of the other girls went for it so I got the job."

"What was he like as a boss?"

"I couldn't have wished for better. He was really considerate and when he saw I could do the work he paid for me to go to college one day a week to get a qualification. I learnt shorthand, typing and bookkeeping."

"How many people were in the office?"

"Oh, only me. He was just getting started again. He'd sold his builder's business and was investing the proceeds. There wasn't a lot to do at first but he'd rented a small one-room office and I just answered the phone and one or two letters a day and brewed up.

"It gradually got busier as word got around and all sorts of people started contacting him. Before I left he'd already moved into a bigger office in the town centre."

"Was his wife still with him?"

Christine Clarke looked surprised at this question.

"I don't know," she said. "It was nothing to do with me. I learnt later that they had broken up but I don't really know quite when it happened. His wife never came into the office but why would she? I don't think she was ever mentioned."

"So you were in the office alone with him?"

"I was actually in the office on my own for a good deal of the time but he did come in every day at some point or another. Why?"

"Did Mr Jones ever make improper advances towards you?"

Mrs Clarke gasped.

"Of course not," she said indignantly. "It wasn't like that. He wasn't a cradle snatcher."

For the first time her husband spoke.

"You think Becky is his, don't you," he demanded. "She was a honeymoon baby. She is very definitely all ours."

Amos held up his hands in appeasement. He thought that most people exaggerated supposed family resemblances but now he looked properly for the first time he could see that the little girl undoubtedly shared her father's facial features.

"I'm really very sorry if I have offended you," he said, "but I do need to find out all I can about Mr Jones if I am to catch his killer. He seems to have one or two admirers. Did he pursue <u>them</u> or did they pursue <u>him</u>?"

Christine Clarke seemed satisfied with this apology.

"I think pursuing is too strong a word. Mr Jones certainly had charisma and charm but I don't think he set out to break hearts. He was a really decent bloke but, as I came to realise towards the end of my time working for him, he was still in love with his wife. There was always a barrier between him and the other women in his life."

"This is really helpful, Mrs Clarke," Amos said encouragingly. "Did a woman called Sarah Miles ever come to the office? Was she one of the other women in his life?"

"She did call occasionally, usually on a Friday for some reason. I assume that was when she was in Horncastle – I think she lived in a village a few miles out but I'm not sure. I didn't take much notice. But I do remember it was usually a Friday because she always asked Mr Jones what he was doing on Sunday.

"She was a funny woman, a bit mousy most of the time but just occasionally she looked as if she was about to blow up. Mr Jones always steered her out of the office as quickly as possible.

"He knew he could leave me to deal with things," she added proudly. "I think they went to a cafe in the market square because I saw them in there once or twice when I locked up and went for my lunch."

"I take it," Amos said, "That Jade Nolan was a fairly recent recruit. Was she taken on because business was expanding?"

"Yes and no," Mrs Clarke responded. "We were expanding, yes, and Mr Jones wanted to take on an office junior under me with me as office manager. I'd just got engaged to Ken and we wanted to start a family straight away so I didn't think it was fair for me to take the manager's job and then let Mr Jones down.

"Eventually he realised he wasn't going to change my mind so he brought in Jade Nolan as manager because she already had some office experience and I showed her the ropes. When I left I think they took on another girl from school as a junior."

"How did you get on with Miss Nolan?"

"Fine. We hit it off pretty well. She soon realised I wasn't a rival for her job."

"And did she realise you weren't a rival for Mr Jones's affections?"

Christine Clarke smiled.

"You'd noticed? Yes, she had a soft spot for Mr Jones and he was really very kind to her even though she was, well, a bit brusque with Miss Miles when she popped in.

"I don't think there was anything in it on Mr Jones's side. In fact, I'm sure there wasn't. It's just that he was a very tactile person. He'd touch your arm or put his hand on your shoulder and he always helped a lady on with her coat or held the door open for her."

"Do you know if he ever saw Jade Nolan outside the office?"

"Not while I was there, as far as I know, but we didn't overlap for long. I did hear that he took her to business events like the Chamber of Trade annual ball but I'm sure he always behaved as a gentleman."

"I want to ask you something very important," Amos said leaning forward. "Were you working for Mr Jones when he was involved with a company called Wardle & Berry?"

Mrs Clarke shook her head.

"I remember the company," she said. "My Dad used to get stuff from there for DIY. I think Mr Jones was involved in some way because there was talk that he made money out of it and that was one reason he could afford to set up his investment business.

"I didn't take much notice because I was still at school. Dad used to bang on about it. He was a bit annoyed he had to get his DIY stuff from somewhere else. It's a pity you can't ask him but he died when Becky was just three months old."

"Did a man called Jim Berry ever come to Mr Jones's office while you were working there?"

"Oh, yes, Jim Berry. Was he the Berry in Wardle & Berry? It never clicked. But it couldn't have been. Jim Berry was quite scruffy. I was surprised Mr Jones allowed him in the office. He always used to whisk him straight through into the back.

"I dreaded the thought that he might come in when I was on my own but he never did. Luckily, Mr Jones was always in the office when he called. It was almost as if Mr Jones was expecting him to turn up.

"It was typical of Mr Jones that he always raided the petty cash for him. I'm not a believer myself, like Mr Jones was, but that's what I call a true Christian, helping those in need."

Amos and Swift took their leave and headed back to Horncastle police station ready to mount the search of Berry's home but things had not gone according to plan. There was no warrant and no team to conduct the search.

The senior officer in charge said he did not have the manpower after lending three officers to collect the files from Ray Jones's office and to make matters worse he had taken the precaution of getting the Chief Constable's support.

Amos and Swift spent a desultory couple of hours going through Jones's files without turning anything up before deciding to call it a day and get the warrant themselves the following morning.

"Berry can wait until tomorrow," Amos said on the way back to their homes in Lincoln. "He isn't going anywhere and he doesn't know we're onto him. If he is the murderer, he can't hide the weapon because he left it at the scene and if he needed to get rid of any blood splattered clothing he's had plenty of time to do it already."

However, it so happened that Amos was distracted from this proposed action for somewhat longer than he intended.

Chapter 17

"There's a woman waiting to see you, sir," a uniformed policewoman remarked as Amos walked into Lincolnshire police headquarters at Nettleham, near Lincoln, on his way from home to Horncastle next morning.

"It's in connection with the murder inquiry," the obliging young officer continued. "It's Mrs Jones. She's in interview room one with Sgt Swift."

Amos was completely taken aback. Inquiries so far had revealed the existence of a wife but not of her whereabouts. Now she had appeared from nowhere.

Cursing his tardiness in arriving at HQ, he bustled into the interview room just in time to hear Swift asking: "Is there any chance, Mrs Jones, that you can give us some clue as to where your husband might have been intending to go on Sunday afternoon?"

Amos was not hopeful. After all, the couple had been living apart, probably miles apart, for the past few years.

"I don't know where he might have been going."

There was a slight pause. Something about the gentle stress on the word "might" caused the inspector to raise his eyebrows.

"But I do know where he should have been," Mrs Jones continued archly. "He was supposed to visit me."

Amos dropped the pen he had just taken out of his pocket onto the table.

"You?" he asked in a startled tone.

"Me."

Amos eyed her as she paused for effect. She was striking rather than beautiful, tall, blonde and dressed in sharp but not gaudy colours. Her clothes were good quality and although they did not boast the cut of designer labels they were at least Marks & Spencer.

Mrs Jones sat calmly and spoke in a matter-of-fact way, clearly relishing the stir she was causing.

Recovering his own composure and belatedly introducing himself, Amos said: "I think you'd better tell me all about it. Shall we start with when you arranged to see your husband and why."

Mrs Jones sat up, leaned forward over the desk and began.

"The arrangement was made the previous Sunday evening. Ray had rung me and asked if we could try to get back together again. I told him I was willing to talk things over but I wasn't prepared to commit myself."

"Were you in regular contact?" Amos interposed.

"Frequent, but not regular," Mrs Jones replied pedantically. "We talked on the phone from time to time but there was no set arrangement."

"So you were still on good terms with your husband despite the separation?"

"Yes. There was no bitterness when we broke up. It was more in sadness than in anger. Ray got completely absorbed in his work. It got to the point where he was wheeling and dealing six, even seven, days a week.

"He couldn't bear to go on holiday in case he missed out. I started to go away for the odd week to the Isle of Wight or the Lake District and he would join me at the weekend. Or not as the case may be.

"Finally he had a heart attack. I thought this would be a lesson to him. Not a bit of it. Even from his hospital bed he was organising his investments. As soon as he was well again he was back in the thick of things. Only now he had religion as well.

"Looking death in the face had certainly shaken him. He started going to church every Sunday evening. He'd never been in the place before in his life. I gave him an ultimatum. The church I could stand – at least it was only once a week. But either he cut back on work or I left him.

"He eased up a bit but it wasn't much more than a gesture. Then came the final straw: The night of the ice cream chimes."

Mrs Jones was clearly enjoying her role centre stage. She paused for effect once again. If she was hoping that Amos would indulge her with a prompt, however, she was doomed to disappointment. He simply stared her down, watching her every facial expression.

Finally Mrs Jones looked away.

"The ice cream chimes," she picked up the thread again. "I didn't always go to church with him – I'm not a believer, any more than Ray was before he realised he might face the Almighty sooner rather than later. But I was there that Sunday evening, I'm sorry to say.

"Well, in the middle of prayers an ice cream van arrived across the road and started playing *How much is that doggie in the window?* It was quite funny, really. Several people couldn't stop themselves tittering. It certainly made me giggle. Not Ray. He got up pompously and ostentatiously and left the pew. He had to get past two or three people to do so.

"He walked imperiously out of the church and a few moments later the chimes stopped abruptly. It was a hot evening – hence the ice cream van – and the doors and the top windows were open. We could hear the ice cream van driver shouting at Ray as he walked back to the church: 'You're not a police inspector. You're Ray Jones. I'll report you for impersonation.'

"Then the van revved up and drove off. I've never heard screeching from an ice cream van's tyres before or since.

"Everyone was sniggering behind their clasped hands. No-one dared to look at Ray in case they burst out laughing. I felt completely humiliated. Talking about it now, it all sounds very trivial but for me it was the last straw. It was typical of the way he expected other people to suit him. Next day I carried out my threat and left him.

"I went to Nottingham because I had friends there. I took a job back in teaching and bought a small flat. I asked Ray for as little money as possible – just a few hundred for the deposit and to live on until my first month's salary was through. I didn't want anyone to say I'd been sponging off him."

Mrs Jones stopped again. "Can I have a drink, please?" she asked.

"Tea ... coffee ... orange squash?" Amos asked as he rose to his feet. He was not sorry for a short break at this point while he digested the insight that the woman across the table had given him into the life and times of her dead husband.

Chapter 18

Amos wandered out of the interview room and was relieved to see his friend Sgt Mark Jenkins at the desk.

"It's getting interesting," Amos remarked. "Any chance you could spare someone to get tea?"

"Do I get a mention in dispatches?" Jenkins asked with a grin.

"Happen," Amos replied noncommittally. He was glad of the diversion created by this banal conversation. It gave him the few moments' break he needed to digest the unexpected appearance of Jones's wife and to put the many questions he wanted to ask into some semblance of order.

Nor did he want to sound too eager to hear what Mrs Jones had to say. He neither wanted to put her off nor to put her on her guard.

A constable whom Amos had never seen before was despatched to the canteen for refreshments.

A couple of minutes was enough. Two beakers of tea duly appeared – real tea, Amos noted with approval, not the brown stuff out of the machine down the corridor. Amos always selected white coffee on the rare occasions that he used the machine because that tasted passably like tea. The tea tasted like nothing in particular.

This was a good brew. Even Mrs Jones sipped it appreciatively. She and Amos sat in silence for a few moments but the officer, having had his brief respite, was now impatient to continue.

Sensing his shuffling, Mrs Jones looked him in the face and raised her eyebrows quizzically to signal that she was ready to resume.

"How did you feel about your husband? What sort of relationship did you have?"

Amos was flustered as he tried to ask the question he particularly wanted answered. His Baptist upbringing still left him prudish after all these years.

Finally Mrs Jones took the hint.

"Are you trying to ask me if I had sex with my husband when I lived with him?" she inquired without embarrassment, indeed with a touch of humour in her voice.

"Well, yes," Amos said. "How did you feel towards him?" He blushed slightly.

"It's difficult to explain," the woman opposite him began. "I was very fond of him, certainly. Do you believe love is the basis for any marriage?" she asked suddenly.

Amos was certainly blushing now.

"I thought that was the general idea," was the best he could manage.

"If you love your partner it's certainly a bonus," Mrs Jones went on unabashed, "but it's not the basis of marriage. Marriage is a working relationship. Not quite a business arrangement – that's too cold. But certainly a working relationship.

"Yes, I did love him once, before we were married – and afterwards. But you have to get on together, make compromises, share interests."

This Amos understood. He had much the same relationship with his own wife. His work had made a long-term passion unrealistic. The long irregular hours, bad enough when he was a constable on shifts, had got no better as he climbed the ladder, each higher rung bringing its own demands. However many people you have to give orders to, you are always at someone else's beck and call.

"I understand," he replied simply.

"I don't think Ray ever had an affair," Mrs Jones picked up. "I'm sure he didn't. He was too tied up with his ever-increasing business empire.

"Empire!" she repeated with a dry laugh. "He was a giant carp in a little puddle. Well, it's all history now but, as I told you earlier, we rather started to lead separate lives. It was all pretty amicable, no bitterness, no hard feelings.

"I actually admired him for his achievements. Some of the business people we entertained were real snobs but Ray told them his mother had gone out cleaning when the family store went through a bad patch to give her three children a better chance in life. They all went to university. Ray was the middle one. He was at Leeds studying psychology. He realised it helped him in his business dealings.

"Anyway, Ray pursued his business career and I finally went off to Nottingham. We kept in touch. Infrequently, but in touch."

"Did you have children?"

"No. We never found out for certain why not. There was nothing physically wrong with me. Ray wouldn't go for tests. It was unspoken between us but I think we both assumed the problem was with him. That was one reason why he threw himself more into the business.

"He gradually lost interest in sex. By that stage I wasn't too bothered anyway because it was clear that our relationship was going no further."

Amos leaned forward. "The Sunday he was supposed to see you," he said. "How did that come about? Who got in touch with whom?"

"Ray rang me," Mrs Jones replied. "In fact, he got in touch the previous week. We hadn't spoken for quite a while when he rang up and said he wanted to see me."

"And he never turned up," Amos mused thoughtfully.

"Yes he did," the women opposite butted in quickly. "At least, he did on the first Sunday. He came to see me and we had a chat over tea and chocolate éclairs. It was all very civilised."

Mrs Jones inserted another of the pauses she made for effect. She knew she was putting a whole new light on the investigation and she was quite relishing her power.

She's not all that upset about her husband's death, Amos thought. Sad, but not grief stricken.

Amos let the silence roll on, hoping for the psychological victory of making Mrs Jones continue her story unprompted.

More tea had arrived with a plate of digestive biscuits. Not quite up to chocolate éclairs standard, Amos thought, but after all this was only police canteen fare. They sipped the tea, still in silence. It was Amos who cracked.

"What did you talk about over ..." he looked ruefully at the biscuit in his hand "... over your dairy cream éclairs?"

"As I said earlier, Ray wanted me to come back to him. He said we made a great couple despite our differences. In fact, he said it was the differences that made life interesting. He couldn't promise to give up his business deals – at least he was honest about that – but he promised there would be no more embarrassments.

"No more Sunday nights at the ice cream van, no more quiet drinks in a dark corner of the pub with Jim Berry while I sat on my own at another table, no more public squabbles with the reporter from the local paper.

"He meant it. Whatever his faults, Ray kept his word whether it was a promise or a threat. He didn't use words lightly. It was one reason why he was so successful at business. People he dealt with knew they could trust him.

"He stood by his word even if it cost him. And he looked after those who were loyal to him. So I knew precisely what terms I would be coming back on."

Amos was temporarily distracted by the re-emergence of Jim Berry, the man who featured so persistently in Jones's business files and who had looked to be emerging as the prime suspect the previous evening.

It was Swift who picked up on what Mrs Jones was saying.

"Terms?" she asked. "A working arrangement, I suppose?"

There was a hint of scorn in Swift's voice but the matter-of-fact woman opposite either failed to detect it or chose to ignore it.

"Yes, a working arrangement," she replied. "Ray didn't push me. He suggested I thought about it and we would meet again in a week's time."

"Except that the next week he didn't turn up," Amos said. "Didn't you wonder why? Didn't you try to contact him? There was no message from you on his answering machine."

"No. I waited in but I just assumed that some business had kept him. Reverting to type, you might say. By 4 o'clock I just cleared away the cups and saucers. I ate my cream cake and put his back in the fridge."

"And what was your answer going to be ... if he had turned up?"

"I was sad in a way when he didn't show up. I certainly felt slighted. But I was also a bit relieved, to be honest, because it made my mind up for me. Our relationship went back into the fridge along with his cake."

"Did you not feel tempted to ring Mr Jones to find out why he failed to turn up?" Amos persisted. "Surely you were surprised. After all, he had gone to the trouble of contacting you and had travelled all the way to Nottingham to ask you back. You must have wondered what had happened to him."

"Of course I did," Mrs Jones replied almost petulantly, "but I wasn't giving him the satisfaction of having me chase after him. Like I said, I wasn't sure I wanted to come back anyway and when he left me sitting twiddling my thumbs I certainly wasn't going to the bother of ringing him.

"It was up to him to get in touch and make his apologies. Not that Ray ever did apologise. I assumed he had put some business deal before me. In that case I knew my place – and it was not back with him. I told myself he'd done me a favour."

Amos shifted in his chair. He had a bad habit of leaning back and sliding imperceptibly down and under the table as he listened, especially when the person being interviewed was willing to talk at length.

The inspector pulled himself up and leaned over the desk.

"When did you find out what had happened to your husband? Who told you?"

Mrs Jones smiled. "I still have a great affection for Lincolnshire. I found it painfully quiet, yes, but at least you could walk around at night and feel safe."

She shuddered slightly, realising what she had said. They were discussing a man who had not been able to sleep safely in his own bed, never mind walk the streets.

"Well, that's how I think of the place, anyway. And I know a lot of people in the county. Most I met through Ray's business deals but I had plenty of personal friends as well. I didn't sit at home being a cabbage. I joined the local bridge club and the history society. I had time on my hands when Ray was out wheeling and dealing. I told you at the start, by the time Ray and I split up we were leading pretty well separate lives."

"So a friend got in touch?" Amos ventured. "I'm surprised no-one contacted you right away. Or perhaps they did."

"Not a friend, exactly. I lost direct contact with a lot of people here when I left. Remember, the intention was to make a fresh start in a new place.

"No, the friend, if you like, was the local weekly paper. I pay an annual subscription and they post it to me. As you can imagine, the latest edition was a bit of a stunner. It arrived in yesterday's post."

"Why did you wait until today to come forward?" Amos demanded.

"I nearly didn't come forward at all," Mrs Jones replied quite sharply. "Why should I? Ray's death was nothing to do with me."

"But you decided to do your civic duty," Amos said coldly. "Or did you decide to claim your inheritance? It must be a tidy sum."

Mrs Jones was quite put out. "I have come here voluntarily," she said curtly.

"Nonetheless," Amos pressed, "You presumably expect to gain something, possibly everything. Surely you are entitled to half anyway as his wife."

"How do I know what's in the will? He could have changed it a dozen times and I wouldn't know. I should imagine he has left me something but I can manage one way or another."

Mrs Jones made one of her pauses for effect. Amos was caught out again. He had slid down the chair into that slouching position. Quickly he pulled himself back up.

"Perhaps he's left it all to that Sarah Miles woman," Mrs Jones went on in an amused tone of voice and with a twinkle in her eye. "She certainly pestered him enough."

Amos attempted to contain his excitement. "Are you implying that your husband was having an affair with Miss Miles?"

Mrs Jones's amusement turned into a laugh.

"I don't think Ray could have stood it. She nearly drove him batty as it was. No, I don't think they were having an affair. They knew each other at church. I knew her as well, of course. She's been the organist for donkey's years.

"Oh, she's a harmless enough soul, I suppose, and most of the time she's quite tolerable. But she can be very intense. She can't let go, like a terrier with a rag doll. I'm sure she saw her chance with Ray when I left him. He told me she was always fussing round him. Then she would have the sulks when she found she was getting nowhere. It all went round in circles.

"If Ray had a fling with anyone over the past four years – and he as good as admitted it to me on the Sunday he did turn up – it certainly wasn't with Sarah Miles."

At this stage Amos was reluctant to point out the inconsistencies in Mrs Jones's story. While she was willing to keep talking, it was better to let her. There would be time to go through it all in closer detail another time.

"Did he indicate any names?" Amos asked without much hope.

The answer was negative, as he expected.

"I preferred not to know," Mrs Jones added. "We were talking about us, not other relationships that didn't mean very much anyway. Supposing I had gone back to him. I didn't want to bump into some acquaintance in the street and think she had gone to bed with my husband while I was away. I preferred not to know."

"But he did talk about Sarah Miles," Amos interposed. "Did he indicate what terms they were on when he saw you?"

"It was sulk time," came the instant reply. "In fact, it had been rather unpleasant at church on the previous Sunday. I know Ray was very apprehensive about what her attitude would be at the service that evening. I never found out what happened. Ray was going to tell me at our next meeting but, as you know, he didn't turn up."

"Did he say if Miles had threatened him?" Amos asked.

"Well, sort of," Mrs Jones replied. "Apparently she told him on several occasions in no uncertain terms that if she couldn't have Ray no-one else would. But he didn't take it seriously. She would never have killed him. She would probably have settled for a scene in public. That's why Ray was apprehensive about going to church on the weeks when all was not sweetness and light."

"He mentioned this on the previous Sunday?"

"He mentioned it any time we spoke over the past four years, which was probably about a dozen times in all. He put a particularly caustic comment on the last Christmas card. You can see it if you want. I always keep them until the next year so I can remember who to send to. I haven't got it with me but I can post it to you."

"Yes, please," said Amos. "It might be useful even if, as you say, she didn't really mean any physical harm."

They sat in silence for a few moments once more but this time the interview had run its course.

Finally Amos said: "Thank you, Mrs Jones, for coming forward voluntarily. We do have your address, I take it? I shall almost certainly need to talk to you again. And the Christmas card. I should like that, please."

"I shall send it to you at the station here first class. It will be in tonight's post. Your sergeant has my address."

With that Mrs Jones rose to her feet and stretched out her hand. Amos took it, shook it, and opened the door. Mrs Jones sailed through serenely and off out into the street.

Chapter 19

"I'm rapidly losing interest in Jim Berry," Amos told Swift.

"I agree," she replied readily. "If he was going to kill Jones he'd have done it ages ago. And I'm rapidly losing my conviction that the murderer was a man. It could have been, but if love rather than money was the motive then several women are potentially in the frame."

Swift was driving along the A158 towards Horncastle. They had intended calling at the incident room but Amos decided they should head for the village where Ray Jones had met his end.

"The vicarage," Amos remarked casually as they approached their destination. "It's time we had a word with the vicar."

"You won't find him at the vicarage," Swift returned. "It isn't a vicarage any more."

"Of course!" Amos exclaimed. "I should have known. Everything is vanishing from rural Lincolnshire – banks, shops, vicarages."

"It was a damp, rambling old place with dry rot," Swift explained. "Thornley refused to move in when he took over the parish. He persuaded the Church of England to buy him a smaller place that didn't take as much heating. There's only him and his wife. His family are grown up and have left home. The Church was only too happy to agree to his request as it sold off the old vicarage for a tidy sum. It's been done up."

"A bit like Killiney Court," said Amos. "How come you know so much about Thornley? You didn't say you went to his church. In fact, I didn't think you went to any church."

"I don't. But I did make inquiries when this case blew up. It's quite a large church with a decent sized congregation all things considered.

"And yes, it is like Killiney Court – the same development company bought the vicarage."

Swift paused in the conversation as she turned the wheel. The church was already in sight. As the two detectives drove down the High Street, Amos glanced up and spotted the house sign The Old Vicarage. The building behind showed the unmistakeable marks of a modern makeover.

Swift carried on past it, past the church and past the road junction just beyond. She took the next turning on the left and pulled up in front of a non-descript terrace house on the right hand side of the road.

As she and Amos got out of the car, a man wearing a dog collar and accompanied by a woman emerged from the house. They were in their mid 50s and were showing the first signs of approaching old age. Both were greying and they moved at no more than a moderate pace, so Swift, whose door was next to the kerb, had no difficulty in stepping out of the car and intercepting them.

"Mr Thornley?" she inquired of the man.

"Yes. Is it urgent? My wife and I are off to the Mothers' Union meeting," the object of her question replied anxiously. "Can it wait until I've done the opening prayers?"

Amos was alongside them now. He showed his warrant card and was about to request an immediate interview when Thornley turned to his wife and informed her: "Could you explain, dear, and take the prayers? I'm sorry, but it is a long time since I missed."

Mrs Thornley sighed. The corners of her mouth turned up in a waspish gesture rather akin to a petulant shrugging of the shoulders.

"They won't be pleased," she snapped. "You know how much they enjoy having you there."

Thornley made no reply. His wife, seeing that further entreaties were pointless, turned and walked off up the street and round the corner as hastily as her years would allow.

"At least I won't have to put up with that ghastly dirge they always want to sing," the vicar suddenly blurted out as soon as she was out if sight. The vehemence took Amos and Swift aback.

"*Make Me a Channel of Thy Peace*," the vicar explained, now speaking more in sorrow than in anger. "They're nearly all old and they act old even if they're not but they think they are trendy singing a supposed hymn that doesn't scan, let alone fit the tune. Mrs Price can't play the piano properly.

"It's bad enough with a proper accompaniment. You can't imagine the discordant chaos without one."

Only now did Amos fully recognise the careworn look in the vicar's face and the hunched shoulders that seemed to carry all the sins of the world upon them.

"Come inside," Thornley said resignedly as he took out his key and opened the front door. He stepped inside and then flattened himself as best he could for a man of middle-aged stomach dimensions to let the other two through the narrow hallway.

They completed the manoeuvre with some difficulty. Amos and Swift moved down the passageway while Thornley closed the front door. The officers were hesitating between two doors, one on the side of the passage and the other at the far end.

"Through here," said Thornley as he squeezed himself between the officers and a row of coats on a rack to reach the front of the line again. He opened the far door and led the way into a small kitchen-diner.

"Then they will want a consoling prayer to end so they can all go home feeling warm and smug," Thornley suddenly remarked bitterly.

The vicar hastily gathered up various religious texts from a couple of chairs and dumped them onto the table. The three occupants of the room sat down on the newly freed kitchen chairs round the now encumbered table.

"Sorry about the mess," Thornley suddenly bumbled. Then, half rising, he added: "I'd better clear this up."

"Sit down, Mr Thornley," Amos said politely but firmly. "We don't need the table. Tell us about Raymond Jones. Who did he know at church?"

"Who didn't he know? Some were friends, some were business contacts. He must have been acquainted with just about everyone in the congregation to a greater or lesser extent."

"How well did you know him?"

"He was a parishioner and a regular churchgoer. He helped with various functions from time to time. I can't say he was a close friend, but he was steadfast and reliable. Those are rare virtues these days."

"Did he know anyone in particular? Who did he talk to after the service?" Amos persisted. He was starting to get exasperated and it was beginning to show.

"Well, he knew Sarah Miles, the organist," Thornley responded. "She was the one who found him, you know. Well yes, of course you know. She was always fussing round him.

"They talked a lot – when they were on speaking terms, that is, which was about half the time. He used to go up to the organ after services and talk to her when he wasn't scurrying off to avoid her. They met occasionally for coffee or afternoon tea at a café in the town, I believe."

Thornley had a sudden thought. "I don't believe there was any impropriety in their relationship. In fact, I'm sure there wasn't. Anyway, I don't listen to idle gossip."

"You seem to know an awful lot about their ..." Amos hesitated for half a second "... friendship."

"I should do. I heard enough about it. On the days when Mr Jones was out of favour with Miss Miles she came to me. I heard all about it. At length."

"It sounds like a very close relationship," suggested Amos with a slight emphasis on the word close. "Was it a romantic, albeit chaste, attachment?"

"It was hardly romantic." The response came almost in an explosion. "Love-hate, maybe, but there was nothing romantic about it. Ray was hardly the romantic type and Sarah was well past the age of fairy tales.

"I doubt if she'd ever been taken out by a man – not on a proper date. She was hardly likely to expect a Prince Charming to come riding over the hill on a white charger. Still, you never know. We all live in hope."

Now that it was too late to sally forth to save the souls of the local mothers, Thornley had time on his hands and he was gradually getting quite voluble.

"Sarah saw the chance of a comfortable life, being a respected member of the community instead of a lonely old spinster with people sniggering behind her back about her not being able to get a man."

The vicar checked himself, realising that he was becoming rather careless in what he said.

"You seem to feel very strongly about it," Amos remarked dryly. He saw that the vicar was hesitating and hoped to provoke him into indiscretions.

Thornley spoke more slowly now.

"It saddens me greatly," he said with a sigh, "that people who profess to be Christians can be rather unfeeling. Sarah has been a great servant of God and this church. Heaven knows where I would get another organist from if anything happened to her."

Amos saw to his regret that the clergyman was going to be more discrete with any further insights into Sarah Miles's character.

"How did she get to know Ray Jones so well? Was it through mutual faith?"

"They met originally at church, I believe. It was before I became vicar here. But it went beyond that. Mr Jones helped her out when she was in financial difficulties.

"She paid him back as soon as she could," Thornley answered hastily. "Sarah was extremely grateful. It was fine until Mrs Jones left him. Then the roller coaster began."

Thornley again checked himself.

"Where was the roller coaster in the last two weeks of Mr Jones's life? Up, down, or somewhere in between?"

"I really don't know. It hardly matters. Ray told me he was talking to his wife about getting back together so it was all immaterial, though he told me not to tell Sarah. I didn't want to get involved so I kept well out of it."

"You knew Jones was in contact with his wife?" Amos asked in surprise.

"He saw her the Sunday before he died and he was going to see her the following Sunday."

Amos was incredulous. "You knew he had seen his wife days before he died? Why on earth didn't you come forward straight away to tell us?"

"Nobody asked me," Thornley protested self-righteously. "You knew where I was if you wanted to talk to me. Is it important that Mr Jones was seeing his wife? It isn't a crime."

Amos saw little point in stating how keen he had been to know Jones's movements so he contented himself with asking: "How did you know?"

Thornley raised an eyebrow to indicate that he did not know what all the fuss was about.

"Sarah Miles told me a couple of days ago."

"Sarah Miles knew Ray Jones was visiting his wife," Amos asked with growing incredulity. "Yet he was apparently keeping the purpose of his visit secret from her. How did she feel about him seeing his wife on two consecutive Sundays? She must have suspected something. From what you have told us she can hardly have been best pleased."

"I don't suppose she was. I really don't know. After she told me I kept well clear."

"How was she on the Sunday – the Sunday Jones was supposed to see his wife for the second time?"

"A bit distracted. She played one or two wrong notes, which wasn't like her at all. But otherwise she seemed quite calm."

"And at the end of the service?"

"I assume she went home. She left immediately after playing the recessional."

A sudden thought struck Amos.

"Your wife," he asked. "Is she by any chance called Joan?"

"Well, yes," Thornley replied cautiously. "Is that relevant to anything?"

"It may be," Amos said enigmatically. "Do you by any chance know Kate Leach? Is she a member of your congregation?"

"No," Thornley said perfunctorily. "I know all my congregation personally."

"You would know this woman," Swift ventured. "She is in her early 20s, unmarried and heavily pregnant. She lives in Killiney Court."

"Still no," Thornley replied easily.

Swift persisted: "Perhaps Mrs Thornley knew her. Maybe visited her to offer support. Could she have gone there last Friday when Miss Leach was very close to going pop."

Thornley ignored the crude euphemism for giving birth.

Instead he replied with the hint of a wry smile: "Supplying succour to an unmarried mother who wasn't even a parishioner? I somehow doubt it. Anyway, she certainly didn't visit her on Friday. We were together all day. My wife helped me with my sermon for Sunday in the morning and we visited hospital in the afternoon. Visiting genuine deserving cases," he added with a hint of sarcasm.

Amos rose. "Thank you for your time – and for sacrificing your moments with the ladies of your parish," he remarked.

Thornley looked without success to see if Amos was genuinely thanking him or being sardonic.

As the officers were leaving, Amos turned suddenly and inquired: "Is the church left locked?"

Thornley looked lightly apprehensive. He clearly did not know quite how to take Amos.

"Yes, usually," he replied, "but my wife should still be there with the ladies' group. If they've finished early, the key is at number 75, the house next door."

As they got into the car, Swift also looked slightly puzzled. "What do you expect to find in the church, sir?" she asked.

"Nothing in particular," came the reply, "but Jones was a regular churchgoer and so might his murderer have been.

It would be rather remiss not to take the chance of looking inside when we are so close. Besides, Thornley seemed to clamp up suddenly and I wanted to unsettle him."

Chapter 20

Swift drove the short distance back to the church while Amos mused silently. She pulled up outside the caretaker's house but there was no need to go in search of the key, since the church door was ajar.

"Do you think that Thornley was telling the truth about being with his wife all day Friday?" she asked. "I took it you were working on the similarities of the two surnames."

"Bit of a coincidence, Thornton and Thornley," Amos responded. "But no, I don't think that Mrs Vicar was the mystery visitor to Killiney Court on the fateful evening."

The two officers nonchalantly covered the few yards of pathway from the church gate and walked in. There was no obvious sign of life despite the perceived need to keep the church locked when it was empty. The women's group were keeping their disappointment at the non-appearance of their beloved vicar private behind one of the doors leading off from near the rear of the church.

Amos and Swift strolled up the aisle in conversation.

"The thing that keeps coming back to bother me," Amos remarked as he gazed round, taking in the surroundings so familiar to the murder victim, "is why Sarah Miles waited until Tuesday before going round to Jones's flat. If she was so concerned about him, why didn't she check out the apartment on the Sunday?"

"Perhaps she wasn't all that bothered after all," Swift returned.

"She was that," came a slightly indignant voice behind them.

Only now, as they approached the transept, did they notice the vase and bunch of cut blooms lying on the front pew. A few wilting flowers lay alongside.

The woman who now addressed the police officers had come in to refresh the arrangements for the midweek service.

"She was that," the voice repeated firmly.

Amos and Swift turned to see a middle aged woman, dressed in tweedy clothing, carrying a jug full of water. Her attire was past its best, though by no means threadbare.

"You were here on the Sunday night," Amos said as an assertion rather than a question.

"I was that," came the reply. "Are you reporters? I can tell you plenty. How much do you pay?"

"We're not reporters, we're police," Swift responded as she produced her warrant card. "And we don't pay."

The woman looked disappointed.

"As you can tell us plenty, perhaps you would like to make a start," Swift suggested firmly.

The deflated flower lady hummed and ha-ed quite a bit until she got going: "Sarah Miles was a man chaser. She never caught one because she always scared them off. Ray Jones was her last chance and she certainly went for it."

"I understood the relationship had cooled a little," Amos remarked casually, allowing the hope of provoking her to further comments to override a strict adherence to the truth.

"You wouldn't have thought so on Sunday night," came the hoped-for retort. "You should have heard the way she played the Hallelujah Chorus."

"What about the Hallelujah Chorus?" Swift prompted.

"You can always tell when she wants to get away after a service. She switches the organ on full blast and belts it out so we can't stand the deafening racket. Well, she doesn't drive me out of my church. Then she had the nerve to have a go at the vicar."

"The vicar? It was hardly his fault," Amos said in a conciliatory tone.

"Of course it wasn't," snapped the flower arranger. "But she still went on at him about how Mr Jones had told her he would be there for evensong as usual and how concerned she was at his absence.

"I think she wanted Mr Thornley to go round to his flat with her but the vicar likes to get home to relax after the service. He's very dedicated, you know. He works very hard and he's just as much right to go home after work as anyone else."

"Quite so," agreed Amos, attempting to extricate himself and Swift.

However, as they hustled out of the church Amos took the precaution of checking the flower duty list pinned up at the entrance and made a note of the name against that week's date.

As the officers returned to the car Amos remarked: "You know what bothers me most about this inquiry? Everyone is so keen to talk. Usually the more serious the crime is, the more people clamp up. They're scared to get involved. But everyone we've talked to seems keen to implicate someone else. They can't all be innocent."

Swift was already unlocking the car before she realised that her superior remained standing on the pavement, making no attempt to walk round to the passenger door. Mistaking his intentions, she held the driver's door open and stood back to allow him to get in.

However, Amos told her: "Lock up again. It's easier to walk from here."

Five minutes later the two police officers found themselves back in the hamster's cage.

Amos came straight to the point: "Why didn't you tell us that you visited Killiney Court on Friday evening?"

Sarah Miles remained silent, though she looked Amos steadily in the eye.

"You went to Killiney Court on Friday evening," Amos repeated. "Why did you not tell us? You did not sign out again. How long did you stay? All night?"

Again, Miles stared and kept her silence.

"You were caught out by the security guard's signing in book, weren't you? It wasn't there the last time you visited Killiney Court. So you signed the first name that came into your head, which was the vicar's wife, except that half way through you had the presence of mind to alter the surname. And you just stuck in a flat number on a different floor from the one you were really visiting."

The two protagonists held their steady gaze. Amos paused again. Miles maintained her steadfast silence.

Finally, Amos spoke in quiet, deliberate tones: "You went to see Ray Jones on the night he died."

Silently he said to himself: "You can outstare anyone else as long as you tell yourself you can do it. Just like you can always outstare an animal. Because you know you can do it. They don't. They don't. They don't. They don't."

At last, Miles broke first: "So what? So I went round on Friday. He wouldn't answer the door. I know he was in. The lights were on. So was the television. He wouldn't answer. I rang and knocked. So I left. That guard wasn't there when I came out so I just drove back home."

"Or perhaps he let you in and you stayed long enough to kill him. Did you go straight home? What did you do when you got home?"

But that was as far as Miles was going. She sank back into a sulky silence. Finally Amos said wearily: "OK, we're going."

Chapter 21

"Fancy a pint, Sir?"

Constable Jane Wyman always called Sgt Swift "Sir" on duty. They were personal friends outside The Job but Wyman felt a bit of respect was called for, with Swift being a sergeant, and in the CID at that.

"Sarge" sounded too informal and "Ma'am" too formal, and neither were right for Swift. So "Sir" it was.

They were school chums who had joined the force together but in other ways they were quite different. Swift was plain, flat chested and with an ambition to compensate for her physical shortcomings. Wyman was stunningly beautiful, curvaceous but lacked application.

That Swift had made the effort and achieved her well-deserved promotion provoked no envy in the constable.

What did irk her somewhat was that Swift had a longstanding boyfriend whom she now lived with. Wyman, for all her obvious attractions plus the name of a film star, had moved from one shortlived relationship to another, rarely getting past the front door, let alone into bed.

"I feel like a drink and I notice there is a pub just up the road," Wyman remarked.

Swift nodded assent. It was still a bit early to be boozing but it seemed to have been a long day. In fact, it seemed to have been a long week. She would have to get back to Jason but one pint would do no harm.

Swift and Wyman strolled down the driveway from Killiney Court and across the road. The Killiney Arms public house stood on the opposite side and about 30 yards up a slight incline.

It was still early evening after a round of interviewing those residents who had been missed in the initial inquiries. Only a solitary figure sat hunched in a corner of the saloon bar where he could look out of the window. The man's eyes followed the two women police officers as they approached the door of the pub.

As Swift and Wyman leant against the bar ready to order, the lone man slipped out behind them.

The landlord watched him go in some surprise.

"Well, I've never seen that before," he commented.

"Never seen what?" asked a bemused Wyman.

Swift's eyes were on the half empty pint glass left standing on the table by the window.

"I've never known Jim Berry leave a single drop in his glass before. Nor have I known him leave the pub when two pretty girls walked in. He fancies himself as a ladies man, though heaven knows who'd fancy him. Anyone would think he was scared of you.

"Anyway, what can I get you?"

"Bitter?" asked Wyman, turning away from the landlord in her annoyance at being referred to by a complete stranger as a pretty girl. Swift nodded.

"Two pints of bitter, please."

Wyman had turned her mind to the matter in hand – getting the drinks in – but Swift wandered casually over to the window and watched Berry's progress.

The landlord was patently unaware of his new customers' occupation but Berry surely was not. What else could account for him fleeing behind their backs?

He was walking up the hill at a fast pace. Seeing which way Swift was looking, the landlord paused in the middle of pulling the first pint.

"Went up the hill, did he? Something else he never does."

The landlord went back to pulling the first pint, and picked up a second glass.

"A man of habit, is he?" Swift prompted innocently.

"It's simple enough," the landlord went on, allowing the beer to settle. Apart from Berry's drink, it was the first pull of the evening and the beer was on the lively side.

"Berry lives down the hill." Then enigmatically: "The only other place he goes to is across the road and that's downhill as well."

"Killiney Court?" asked Swift innocently. "Isn't that where the murder took place?"

The landlord topped up the second pint, poured a little more into the first one that had now settled, and placed them both on the bar in front of the officers.

"That's £2.50, please."

Don't be hasty, Swift told herself. Don't look too eager. He doesn't know who we are.

An older man, probably into his seventies, grey and badly shaven, walked through the door and limped up to the bar.

"You're not from round here, I take it." The landlord directed his remark to Swift but he was half looking at the newcomer, whom he evidently recognised.

"Evening, Bert. These two ladies were asking if that building across the road was where the murder took place."

He half chuckled with the air of one of superior knowledge.

"Bad do," Bert muttered his opinion with a shake of his head. "I know some folks couldn't abide Ray Jones but you don't wish that on anyone. Beaten over the head with an iron bar. And in his own bed. It isn't right."

The matter had patently been thrashed out at some length in this neighbourhood hostelry in the evenings since the discovery of Jones's body. You can't stop information getting out, Swift thought.

The landlord was not best pleased at having the attention of these two personable young ladies snatched away from him by an old codger. He lifted up the flap on the bar and came out from behind it.

"But what does Jim Berry know about it?" he asked with an overdone air of mystery as he walked across to the window, drawing attention away from Bert.

"He listens plenty and says little – and only then when he is asked. But I reckon he knows more than he lets on."

"You mean the chap who was in the corner and who sneaked off at the sight of a couple of strangers?" Swift asked. "It sounds fascinating."

She was succeeding in massaging the landlord's ego. How does she manage to string them along like that, Wyman wondered with a mixture of envy and admiration.

"He was in here on the night of the murder, that Friday night," the landlord picked up. "You know they didn't find the body until the Tuesday," he went on in a conspiratorial tone, "but they reckon he was killed on the Friday night. Jim Berry was sitting in that very chair by the window on the night of the murder."

"Lots of people were in here that night," interrupted the older man at the bar. "The place was full. Why pick on him?"

The landlord's reasons for singling out Jim Berry were not, however, to be divulged, for at that moment a waspish woman in her forties appeared through a door marked "private".

"Fred," she said abruptly, "we need some pale ales up from the cellar. Why don't you do your job and leave the police to do theirs."

The landlord did not immediately grasp the implication in his wife's statement but she glanced at the two officers and the penny dropped. The landlord tottered off obediently and somewhat crestfallen to the lower regions of his hostelry.

Chapter 22

Amos's meandering, aimless train of thought was broken as he entered County Headquarters next morning. It was difficult to think straight in a murder inquiry, when your wits need to be at their sharpest: long hours and events churning over in the mind conspired against adequate sleep.

Amos had known murder inquiries before, but this one was particularly frustrating. Most murderers he had encountered were very close to the victim.

The commotion in the reception area was therefore particularly unwelcome. Amos veered abruptly right and was half way through the pair of double swing doors that led round to the back of the building and, circuitously, to his own office when he heard his name mentioned. He recognised the voice above the hubbub and his heart sank.

It was tempting to slink away but Amos felt that he owed it to his colleagues in the front office to rescue them so he turned back reluctantly.

"All right, Sgt Jenkins," he said to the figure who was attempting to take charge of the fracas. "Come along, Jason," he added wearily. "In my office."

Jason was an imposing figure, six feet plus tall, blond, handsome and well built. In another age he could have been a young Viking warrior.

It seemed, though, that he had left home hurriedly that morning. A light stubble, slightly darker than his hair, adorned the lower part of his face. He had slipped on a fairly old pair of jeans and thrust his feet into a pair of brown moccasins without wasting time on socks. His shirt proclaimed allegiance to a local Rugby Union club known for its uncompromising play.

This fine specimen of manhood collapsed in tears over the inspector's desk.

"I love her so much," he gasped between uncontrollable sobs. It would have seemed unreal to Amos – indeed, it had done so the first time it happened – but this was at least the third such performance and the officer knew it was only too real.

Jason controlled himself with difficulty. Amos was aware from past experience that it was best to let nature take its course. Then the torrent began.

"She wasn't back until gone 11 last night it's the third time this week I don't know where she is or what she's doing or when she's coming home there's no food in the place I can't manage without her."

The words tumbled out as if in one sentence. Jason took his first pause for breath. A moment later he was on to the earnest pleading.

"Why does she have to be on this case? Why can't she just do burglaries and come home at a proper time? It isn't safe for a woman. You work her too hard. You expect too much of her."

It was time to pause for a second breath. Amos wished the young man was less fit so that he would have to breathe more often. The momentum was building again.

"She had left already when I woke up this morning. I can't live without her, I can't sleep without her, I can't eat without her."

Not much more to go, thought Amos.

Jason slumped over the desk again and shook violently. More sobs, this time without tears, emitted from his body. After a few moments he was still and drained.

Amos walked round the desk and helped him to his feet. Then he gently escorted the young man out through the back entrance in silence and watched him shuffle forlornly out though the gate that the police cars used.

The inspector had not been in his office long before Det Sgt Swift, who had been out interviewing a couple of possible, though not particularly promising, leads burst into his office without knocking. She looked flustered.

"He's gone," Amos said simply.

"They told me at the front desk he was here," Swift said with embarrassment. "I'm terribly sorry, Sir."

Chapter 23

If the owners of the Killiney Arms hoped that they were off the hook, they were disabused of the notion at 10.45 that morning. Swift had informed Amos of the suspicious behaviour of Jim Berry and the allusion of the landlord to his knowing about the murder.

"It isn't much to go on," Swift confessed at the regular morning meeting of the murder team, "but I really did feel there was something going on there. And Berry did figure in all the Jones files we looked at."

Amos was equally frank: "We haven't got very far in any other direction so we might as well give it a try."

Amos was now hammering on the closed, solid front door of the pub. A vacuum cleaner was buzzing away in the background.

Amos knocked again, louder.

"We're not open until 11," came the reply. The face of the landlord's wife appeared at the lounge window. Amos swiftly flashed his warrant card in front of her face. She grimaced.

A few moments later heavy bolts could be heard being withdrawn behind the barricades and the door was opened to reveal the figure of the landlord.

"Thanks," said Amos perfunctorily as he pushed his way past the startled figure and into the pub. Swift followed, leaving the landlord to close the door and follow them.

This time the landlord's wife was in close attendance to protect her husband from over-indulgence in providing unguarded information.

"I understand you have reason to believe that one of your customers knows something about the murder at Killiney Court," Amos said without embroidery. There was a pause. It was the woman who replied.

"All our customers claim to know something about everything," she said tartly. "Not many of them know anything about anything, but it is our job to humour them."

"But Jim Berry seems to know something the others don't," Amos persisted.

The landlord's wife stuck stubbornly to her line. "We don't talk about our customers to strangers. We talk to them, not about them."

"Would you like a drink… or a coffee," the landlord butted in, hoping to defuse the increasingly frosty atmosphere.

"The coffee's not on yet," responded his better half. "And I'm sure the officers don't drink on duty."

"I would prefer to complete this conversation before your first customers of the day arrive," Amos ventured. "No doubt you would prefer not to have police spoiling the congenial atmosphere, either," he added.

The landlord shot a glance at his wife, who went "hmmph," threw her head back and walked out through the door to the private quarters. A moment later the vacuum cleaner could be heard in the drawing room.

"All I'm saying is this," the landlord conceded, "Jim Berry knew Ray Jones, the dead man. Jim did work for him. Odd jobs. He often left here to go across to see Mr Jones in the early evening, get his orders for next day and come back here. Mr Jones rang him in the afternoon so Jim knew if there was anything doing. Jim hadn't had a call that Friday.

Well, there was nothing unusual in that. There wasn't work every day and Jim wouldn't expect anything for a Saturday. But he still went across on the Friday evening, and much later than usual."

"Berry said he was going across to see Jones on the night Jones was killed?" Swift asked.

"No, he didn't say anything. As a matter of fact, he was quiet and moody. But I came out collecting glasses just as he left and I saw him turn into Killiney Court from the window."

"Where does he live?" Swift inquired.

"He lives just down the road," the landlord said sullenly. "It's the only house with a red door."

"Thank you," Amos said graciously, rising from his perch. "We will trouble you no further."

Then after a pause: "For now."

Chapter 24

Jim Berry was shifty, uncomfortable and defiant as he sat across the interview room table at Horncastle police station from Amos and Swift.

He presented a curious picture with ginger eyebrows that twisted up to a point on the edge of his ruddy face. His tweed jacket was old but clean and leather patches adorned the elbows to protect against wear. His checked shirt was beginning to fray at the collar.

The neatest part of him was his goatee beard, ginger to match the eyebrows but showing more white. His hair was greying and receding and was a week or so overdue for a trim.

At a nod from her superior officer, Swift switched on the tape and went through the routine of stating date, time, and those present.

"Can you confirm, Mr Berry, that I have offered you an opportunity to contact a solicitor and you have declined," Amos asked in a matter-of-fact way.

"What do I want with a lawyer?" Berry asked peevishly. "I can't afford one. They're not interested in the likes of me. I don't need one, anyway. I've done nothing wrong. I'm the victim here."

"As you wish," Amos replied smoothly. "I am investigating the murder of Raymond Jones, which took place last weekend. What were your movements between 5pm on Friday and 10 am on Tuesday?"

"Blimey, I can't remember every single minute," Berry exclaimed. He had, however, lightened noticeably.

"I can't remember off-hand where I was earlier on, but I was in the pub all Friday evening – the one opposite Killiney Court, as if you didn't know. Then I went home at closing time and went to bed.

"I'll have to think about the rest of the weekend. I don't think I know what I was doing most of the time. But I did pop into the pub once or twice on Saturday and Sunday. I stayed in bed all day Monday. I felt poorly."

Swift was surprised that Amos did not immediately press him further on his movements, particularly on the Friday evening when the murder, as they now knew, took place. However, Amos was pursuing a different tack.

"Jones bought your company," the inspector said. "Had you known him before that?"

Berry was relaxing further.

"Nope," he said simply.

"So you were not aware that he already had a reputation for aggressive dealing? You weren't worried that he might swindle you out of your business?"

"Mr Jones was a gentleman," Berry blurted out with surprising indignation. "He always played fair, kept his word. He always," Berry put great stress in the word, "had done."

"I thought you said you didn't know him before he took over your company."

Berry was flustered. Amos now discovered why the eyebrows were twisted up to a point. Berry twirled them whenever he got nervous.

"Well, I didn't really know him," he floundered. "We'd done business with him, him being in the same line of business. I didn't actually know him."

"You speak very highly of him," Amos proffered, "Considering what he did to you."

Berry was thrown again.

"What d'ya mean?" he demanded gruffly.

"Your business," Amos said. "Swindled you out of your business."

"He did no such thing," Berry came back indignantly. "It was my partner Dick Wardle who cheated me. If it hadn't been for Mr Jones I'd have been left with nothing. Wardle took the lot and cleared off. But Mr Jones was a gent like I told you. He gave me a bit of cash."

Amos picked up the papers in front of him. "For the purposes of the tape. I am showing Mr Berry documents relating to the takeover of Mr Berry's company by Raymond Jones."

Amos selected several papers, passing them one at a time across to Berry, who glanced up and down them but said nothing and passed them back.

"So?" he asked Amos.

"So, you can't read," the officer announced. "You've no idea what those documents say, have you?"

"Course I do," Berry persisted but he was looking round wildly as if he hoped a door would suddenly open up along one of the bare walls surrounding him.

"Then tell me," Amos suggested quietly, "which of these papers has nothing to do with you and Mr Jones."

Berry sat sullenly, refusing now to even look at the papers.

The point established, Amos moved on: "So you couldn't read the details. How do you know whether the deal was fair or not?"

"Mr Jones explained it all to me. Wardle had taken all the money out of the business. It was hardly worth anything. In fact, Mr Jones said I would be liable for debts that Wardle had run up without me knowing it. He did his best for me like I told you."

Amos pondered this touching declaration of faith for a few moments.

"Mr Jones gave you odd jobs to do, didn't he?" Swift took up the questioning.

"It was nothing much. I didn't have to declare it to the social services, did I?" Berry asked in desperation. "Look can I have a drink? A cup of tea?"

Swift had the bit between her teeth and was all for turning the rack tighter. She was disappointed when Amos demurred without hesitation.

"Of course you can," he responded sympathetically. "Sergeant Swift and I will organise it. We'll be back in a few moments."

Chapter 25

The two officers left Berry alone while they sent for tea and took stock in the corridor out of his hearing.

"I am convinced," Amos said after a few moments thought, "that Berry genuinely believed Jones. He really believes it was just his former partner who swindled him and that Jones actually came to the rescue. Then he relied on Jones for cash handouts to supplement his state benefit."

"If that is right," Swift butted in, "then what motive has he got for murdering Jones? Surely he wanted Jones alive, not dead."

Amos shrugged his shoulders.

"You could be right," he admitted. "Unless Jones had decided not to use him any more. But I must admit that doesn't ring true."

They stood in silence until tea was delivered and the interview was resumed.

"I don't see any reason to involve social security if you cooperate," Amos said smoothly. "I'm not putting the tape back on so nothing you say now can be used against you."

Berry seemed mollified.

"Now tell me about the work you did for Mr Jones."

Berry was wary but he decided to take his chances with Amos.

"Well, they were just odd jobs. Mr Jones needed information before he did his deals and I just made a few inquiries. Asked around, that sort of thing. I had a lot of contacts from my days in business."

"And you were good at it," Amos suggested in a kindly way. "You couldn't write it down but you could keep it all up here where it was a lot safer," he added tapping his head.

"That's right," Berry replied enthusiastically, feeling that Amos understood him after all. "Up here. Mr Jones was very grateful. He said I had a real head for business."

"So you must have visited Ray Jones's flat quite frequently?" Amos prompted. Berry looked shocked.

"Good Lord no," he answered in astonishment. "Mr Jones wouldn't let me visit his flat. Not that you could blame him," Berry added hastily in defence of his casual employer. "His neighbours are a right stuck-up lot. He couldn't have them seeing a scruffy down-and-out like me turning up at his door."

"Are you saying you never visited Killiney Court?" Swift asked.

"Not since they were fitted out. I did a lot of the electrical work while they were being done up but that was early days. The flats were just shells then. It was the last proper job I did," he added wistfully.

"Mr Jones would ring me when he wanted to see me. He'd ring the pub and leave a message. We sometimes met in the pub. None of his snobby neighbours ever went in there.

"They all thought they'd gone up a rung when they moved into Killiney Court."

Berry gave a sardonic laugh.

"So they had. Up one rung in more ways than one."

Amos looked at him curiously. "What do you mean by that?"

"I'm saying no more," Berry suddenly clamped up. "You've got nothing on me. I had no reason to kill Mr Jones. Now can I go home?"

Amos rose wearily to his feet.

"Yes, Mr Berry. Thank you for your cooperation. You may go home."

Chapter 26

Amos and Swift stood gloomily watching Berry walk down the corridor to freedom.

"It can't be helped, Sir," Swift remarked. "There's no real evidence against him and he had no reason to kill Jones – quite the opposite."

Detective Constable John Cooke was coming towards them and brushed past Berry, turning to stare at him after they passed each other.

He hurried up to Amos.

"You're not letting him go, are you?" he demanded impertinently. "It's obviously him."

Amos and Swift stared at Cooke blankly.

"He's left handed," Cooke explained opaquely with an air of triumph. "So was the murderer."

"How do you make that out?" asked the baffled Amos.

"The murderer struck from the left hand side of the bed. Think how you would hold a cricket bat. A left handed person would hold the bar with his right hand at the end, with his left hand further up the bar, the opposite way to a right handed person. He would strike naturally from the left of the bed. That's what the murderer did."

Then, conspiratorially, he added: "Did you notice Berry's face? His beard was trimmed better on the right. And he had shaved better on the right cheek, too. He had cut himself two or three times on the left cheek and there was more stubble.

That's because as a left-handed person he has more control reaching to the right side of his face."

Cooke stood beaming at the other two officers. He was somewhat deflated, and a little disgruntled, when Amos replied: "The murderer struck from the left side because that was the side nearest the bedroom door. He would hardly have walked round the bed in the dark and risked bumping into it."

Nonetheless, Amos was slightly uneasy. There was no way of knowing if Berry wrote left handed as he did not write. The inspector turned brusquely to Swift.

"Let's visit the estate office," Amos suggested. "That last remark of Berry's puzzled me. What was he on about? Why did he suddenly clamp up?"

Amos expected the estate manager to resent police intrusion into his office in addition to his block of flats. The manager, however, took a refreshingly pragmatic line.

"It's as much in my interests as yours to get this matter cleared up as quickly as possible," he told the two detectives.

"Am I right to think, sir, that just one of the former residents of Killiney Court went back in after the refurbishment?"

"That's right, inspector, as far as I know. The place had got pretty run down – in fact, some of the flats were uninhabitable. We spent a lot of money on the block and the apartments are quite exclusive.

"I'm not being snobbish," said the manager, who hadn't sounded at all snobbish until he uttered the disclaimer, "but the sort of people who rent council flats are hardly likely to be in a position to buy at the upper end of the market. Some may well have bought elsewhere after they moved out but not in Killiney Court."

"Yet Miss Norman found the money from somewhere," Swift returned.

"You'll appreciate I can't go into client's personal details but Miss Norman was a woman of comfortable personal means. She originally moved in, I think you'll find, when the council block was in better condition and when she, perhaps, was not so well off.

"Look," he went on confidentially, "I don't think I'm giving any secrets away when I say that Miss Norman came into some money. I believe a relative died some time ago. She probably just hadn't got round to finding somewhere else when we stepped in and solved the dilemma for her.

"She was very fond of her old home, you know. She moved back into the same flat, although of course it had a different number on it. That caused a bit of confusion. She thought we were trying to trick her into moving into the wrong apartment."

The estate manager laughed. Amos was not laughing. He was remembering the odd remark that Berry had made about the tenants moving up a rung.

"Why was the flat number different?" he asked.

"Didn't you know?" came the slightly surprised reply. "Well, no, I suppose there was no reason for anyone to mention it to you. The development company renumbered the floors after the refurbishment. I suppose it was partly to make it clear that this was a very different apartment block from the old council estate.

"I think, also, there was a certain cachet in going over to US-style numbering. So we made the ground floor one, the mezzanine with the caretaker's flat became two and the old English-style first floor became three.

"Miss Norman's flat, formerly 3A, became 5A and so on."

Unaware of the bombshell he had just dropped, the estate manager continued: "Once Miss Norman looked out of the window she was quite satisfied. She could see at once that it was her old flat overlooking the front drive. I suppose she was a bit lonely and liked to see people coming and going."

Amos was already on his feet.

"Thanks," he said. "We might want to talk to you again."

"Is that it?" a startled manager asked.

Amos was already making for the door with Swift in tow.

"That's all for now," the inspector replied without pausing.

"What's the rush?" Swift asked as Amos strode for the outer door to the office car park.

"Stevens," came the sharp response. "Do you realise the implication of what he said?"

They were at the car and Swift had to wait until they were seated in it and moving for the explanation.

"Supposing the murderer made a mistake. Supposing he didn't know the floors had been renumbered. Supposing he was looking for 4A.

"Think about it," Amos went on urgently as he drove off down the road.

"All the floors look the same. The assailant comes up the stairs to avoid meeting anyone in the lift and counts out the floors. He comes out onto the landing and there are four doors, two on the left and two on the right. In front of him the far wall comes up to waist height, topped with railings. Every floor is identical.

"He gets into what he thinks is 4A, makes for the bedroom – remember all the flats on top of each other are the same layout – sees the sleeping figure and beats it to death. The only trouble is, it's the wrong figure."

"You're forgetting something," Swift pointed out. "Even if the murderer did break into the wrong flat he would have realised his mistake as soon as he entered the bedroom.

Remember the table light was on. I know the bulb was fairly dim but you were there when we switched off the main light and closed the curtains. You could see Jones quite clearly.

"The two flats below Jones were both occupied by women. The killer couldn't possibly have mistaken Jones."

"Not if he was the one who switched the light on – after the deed was done. If I'm right," Amos declared, "then Jones was killed by mistake for the occupant two floors down. Joanna Stevens is in serious danger."

Chapter 27

No-one but Amos was pleased about the 24 hour guard he put on Joanna Stevens, least of all the ungrateful recipient of his well meaning intentions.

Swift could not accept Amos's theory. Detective Constable Martin, the first officer to take up the duty, and the other officers who followed him, accepted the inevitable boredom with a bad grace.

The Chief Constable objected to the cost. He was, though, as Amos had expected, reluctant to remove the chaperone after Amos had set the arrangement in place. He did not want the responsibility if anything happened to Stevens.

"Still," he told Amos, "if she cooperates we need to put only one officer on duty at a time. And if she doesn't cooperate we can't do much to help her so we needn't bother trying."

For all this Amos was prepared. What he had not been expecting was the truculent attitude of Stevens herself. Amos and Swift, being close to Killiney Court, had dashed in vain up to Stevens' flat, just in case she had returned home from work.

The lift had been ages coming to take them back to ground level. Amos paced impatiently.

"It never struck any of us as odd that the first level of flats was the third floor," Swift commented without realising that her attempt at calming Amos was only making him more agitated. "We were so busy getting a list of everyone who lived in the building and finding out where they were that weekend that the numbering didn't seem important. I never gave it a moment's thought myself."

The lift rumbled up and took the two officers back to the ground. The sentry unhelpfully said he had not seen Stevens leave that morning but he had not been on duty then.

It came as a relief to reach her place of work and be greeted on the pavement by Martin, who had got there first in answer to Amos's urgent summons.

"She's fine. She was a bit startled when I barged in, though. I think she's assuming you will explain what it's all about, sir."

Stevens was a lone worker in a small office. She was putting some files into a briefcase as Amos entered.

"Now what's all this about?" she asked abruptly. "And can we make it quick? I have an appointment."

"I'm afraid it's rather serious," Amos told her. "Miss Stevens, I have reason to believe that your life may be in danger."

"Nonsense!" Stevens gasped. "Do you think," she started to inject a tone of sarcasm, "do you think someone is working his way round Killiney Court?"

"No, Miss Stevens," Amos insisted. "It is possible that the murderer intended to kill _you_."

"I can't see why," Stevens commented. "All right, I worked for Ray Jones. But I wasn't employed by him. I have my own business and my own clients. I only check the figures. I don't wheel and deal. Why would the murderer want to kill me as well?"

Amos was put on the spot. He was reluctant to divulge his suspicion for two good reasons.

Firstly, it was only supposition, little more than a hunch.

Secondly, there were times in any investigation, especially murder, when it was best to keep some vital pieces of information away from the general public. The murderer could give him or herself away by revealing knowledge of unpublicised facts.

So Amos said simply: "I'm sorry, Miss Stevens, I can't divulge the reason for my suspicion."

"Has Warren ever threatened you?" Swift asked.

Stevens shook her head. "I've not really had much contact with him, even though we live in the same block. I didn't mix with him socially and just called in his office every six months to check the books. He usually made sure he happened to have an urgent reason to be in London whenever he knew I would be calling so it always got delayed a few days. That's why I didn't warn him in advance that I was going to pop in last Tuesday to tear his books apart."

"What about Jim Berry?" Swift asked.

"What, that grubby little man who did Ray's spying for him? I don't think he even knew Warren," Stevens answered, misunderstanding the question.

"I mean, did he have any reason to hate you? Were you, for instance, involved in winding up his old company?"

"That was before my time. Ray wasn't among my clients then. Or Berry for that matter. I can't for the life of me see why he should hold a grudge. Nor did he owe me any favours. I can't see why he would have any reason to like or dislike me."

Amos and Swift suggested other names of residents in Killiney Court but Stevens was clearly getting bored with the exercise. She showed no greater enthusiasm as Amos produced the lengthy list of business contacts of the late and, so far, unlamented Raymond Jones.

She did, however, go to the extent of marking those whom she had had dealings with, roughly half the roll call.

"Please try to think if anyone on this list, or anyone else for that matter, had any kind of grudge against you," Amos urged. "Meanwhile, we will keep a female officer stationed in your flat overnight and an officer will escort you during the day. I can assure you that as soon as we can get proper arrangements in place my officers will be in plain clothes and will exercise the utmost discretion – although it would be far better for your own sake if you went away for a few days."

"Impossible," Stevens said shortly. "Too much work. And how is one person going to protect me? What will they do if someone drives past with a sawn-off shotgun? I just can't see the point. I am perfectly capable of looking after myself. I always have done and I always will."

"If I am right – and I am quite sure that I am – the killer will not strike in such a melodramatic or public fashion," Amos said. "Mr Jones was killed in the utmost privacy and the killer will try to strike when there is no-one around. If he knows we have an officer on duty at Killiney Court and accompanying you he will be deterred.

"Otherwise, he will wish to eliminate his next victim as soon as possible. I intend to publicise the arrangement in the local media.

"Don't worry," he added hastily as Stevens opened her mouth to protest, "I shan't say specifically that we are guarding you. I shall say that we are keeping a guard on Killiney Court itself and shadowing all known close associates of Ray Jones. I daren't spread it too widely or it will lose its effect. The murderer must know he can't get at you until such time as we can track him down."

Chapter 28

Stevens finally accepted the arrangement with a bad grace. Being now late for her next appointment, she preferred to acquiesce rather than prolong the debate. Martin tagged on behind her. Having given way on the general principle, she also conceded that the shadowing officer would normally travel in her car and stay overnight within her flat.

Swift was despatched back to county headquarters in Martin's car to organise a rota with a female officer assigned to the night duties.

"How long do you want the rota drawn up for?" she asked Amos as she was departing.

"Hard to say," he admitted. "Take it for a week and we'll see how we go. I can't see us sorting this one out quickly. Every time we seem to be getting somewhere the net widens again. We don't even know for sure who the target was, let alone the murderer."

Left on his own, Amos found a telephone box and rang Sheila Burns, his contact on the local evening newspaper. Burns had her head screwed on the right way. She could be trusted with a tip-off because she knew if she played fair she would be used again.

"Sheila? Amos. Can we meet quickly? I've an exclusive for you. Will it be in time for the final edition?"

Half an hour later the pair were ensconced in a small café just outside Lincoln. Amos had two cups of tea paid for and on the table when Burns slipped in through the door.

Amos was already talking as Burns yanked her notebook and pen from her coat pocket. She was in her late 20s and talented enough to move on but she preferred the reassurance of her own beat in her home town.

"We have genuine reason to believe that the killer will strike again at Killiney Court," Amos said quietly but firmly. "I have today taken the precaution of installing a police officer in the building during the hours of darkness. I have also ensured the safety of Jones's known business contacts, especially those living in Killiney Court.

"Don't be too direct but you can speculate that this is likely to include Joanna Stevens, who sometime did accounting work for Jones. Hint at Ray Warren being included since Jones invested in his business. But make it clear without being too specific that Stevens is the main one.

"Don't pin all that on me, please. I'm refusing to confirm or deny this but you can take it that what I've told you is true.

"You can quote me as saying something like: 'There is a dangerous and particularly vicious killer out there and we are taking every precaution to see that this person does not strike again' – the usual sort of stuff. Feel free to make something up along those lines, just as long as it's grammatical."

"Are you making any progress in the investigation?" Burns asked.

Amos could hardly blame her for trying to seek out more information.

"It's still early days," he replied without much conviction. "You can say you believe there is a serious suspect but, again, please don't be too specific. A couple of new lines of inquiry have cropped up today and there are people connected with Jones and Killiney Court who will be interviewed again.

"You can say specifically that we have interviewed all the residents of Killiney Court and eliminated those who were away at the time. Also we have been talking to known associates of Jones, both business and religious.

"Get that lot into the final edition and you have an exclusive. I'll hold off Radio Lincolnshire until you've hit the streets. Don't bother checking this out with the police press office, even if you have time. Only you and I know about this."

Burns nodded, took the last remaining mouthful of tea and vanished. She did not let Amos down, for the story made front page lead in the final edition under a "Killiney Court exclusive" banner, adorned with mugshots of Jones and Amos and "By Sheila Burns" in large type.

"Police fear the Killiney Court killer will strike again, I can reveal exclusively. Inspector Paul Amos, who is in charge of the investigation, is believed to have posted an officer at the block of flats throughout the night to prevent a further attack.

"Police are not releasing the names of those they believe could be in danger but any surveillance is likely to target known associates of murder victim Ray Jones. These include Joanna Stevens, who acted as accountant for Jones on several occasions and who also lives at Killiney Court. Another Killiney Court resident who had business dealings with Mr Jones is Scott Warren.

"Amos declines to reveal specific details of the police operation but he did tell me this afternoon: 'We are looking for a particularly vicious killer.'

"His team have interviewed all the Killiney Court residents and eliminated those who were away on the Friday night that Mr Jones was brutally beaten to death. They have also talked to a wider circle of business associates and to worshippers he knew at the church he attended. I can reveal that several will be interviewed again."

The story then recapped details of the murder. Altogether it made an impressive show, more than enough to get the message across. Even if the illiterate Berry was the murderer, he was bound to hear all about it in the pub.

By the time the newspaper was on sale, Amos had had the opportunity to brief the Chief Constable, who took the news gloomily but with slightly more equanimity than Stevens had done.

"The fact is," he told Amos rather unkindly, "the fact is that you are no nearer to solving this crime than you were when you started. You've got one suspect you're not getting any further forward with, and you can't hold him.

"Just remember we can't keep personal bodyguards going indefinitely. The sooner we call this one off the better. Keep me informed."

Chapter 29

Amos's relief at getting everything into place for the protection of Joanna Stevens was short-lived.

He had actually sent Det Sgt Juliet Swift home for the day, seeing no cause to aggravate her boyfriend Jason any further after they had worked for a full week without break, and was about to vacate his office for the evening when an anguished call from Det Constable Martin came through.

"I've lost her, Sir," Martin gabbled down the phone. "She's done it on purpose. I'm stranded. I'm dreadfully sorry, Sir."

"What do you mean, you've lost her?" Amos demanded, though he had a pretty good idea what Martin meant. "Are you talking about Joanna Stevens? You'd better not be."

"I'm afraid so, Sir," the distressed voice on the phone replied. "I went with her to her meeting in Spilsby like you said to do and she seemed perfectly OK with it. She parked in the market square and put a two-hour parking ticket on the windscreen. She said she'd be quite some time so I escorted her to the meeting and waited in another room while she was talking.

After about half an hour I went to the toilet and she must have slipped out while I was there. I didn't realise she'd gone at first until the guy she'd been talking to came out and asked what I was doing still there. He thought I was her chauffeur and couldn't understand why she'd left without me. Neither could I."

"Neither can I," Amos said angrily.

The inspector took a deep breath.

"All right. It's her own fault if anything happens to her. But it had better not. Get back to Horncastle right away."

"I'm stranded, Sir," Martin said plaintively. "She's got the car. Hang on a minute. There's a bus coming. I'll get on it."

The detective constable slammed the phone down quickly before Amos could vent any more anger on him.

Amos rang home to warn his wife he would be late back. She was used to it by now when a murder inquiry was on, though this one had dragged on much longer than most.

Then he got into his car and drove hastily to Horncastle police station. Martin was not there but a few moments after Amos arrived there was a call from the constable, who was in a far better state of mind.

"I've found her," he announced triumphantly. "I'm ringing from the call box in the market square. She's in a café in the square. I can see her parked car as well."

"Has she seen you?" Amos asked urgently.

"No, I'm quite sure she hasn't. She's got her back to the window."

"Who's she with?"

"There's a bloke sitting opposite her. I don't recognise him."

"Stay where you are," Amos ordered. "I'm coming to you."

"Wait, wait," Martin almost bellowed down the phone. "They're coming out. Do I nab her?"

Amos thought quickly.

"No. I've already despatched another officer to join her. You follow the man. If he gets in a car, get his registration number so we can trace him but don't stop him."

Amos rang off and rushed the short distance to the market square.

From the corner of the square he spotted the policewoman detailed to guard Stevens for the rest of the evening getting into her car with her. Martin was nowhere to be seen.

The inspector slowly made his way back to the local police station. A few minutes later Martin returned.

"I followed him home," he announced proudly. "I know where he lives."

Chapter 30

Amos hated conducting interviews in serious cases without being accompanied by Det Sgt Swift. Although he liked to do most if not all the questioning himself, he valued her opinion on the answers and reactions of the suspects and witnesses.

He needed her presence especially now when he would be talking about affairs of the heart, a subject on which she had a greater insight than he. However, so little progress had been made in this case – they did not even know who the intended victim was, let alone who did it – that he determined to talk to Joanna Stevens' male friend immediately.

Why had she been so keen to give Martin the slip? Was she, after all, involved in the murder of Ray Jones and was setting up an alibi for herself or was she merely trying to keep her private life separate from the murder inquiry?

Start with a clean slate, Amos told himself as he approached the door that Martin pointed to. As soon as the occupant opened the door and Martin identified him as Stevens' mystery man, Amos sent the constable home.

Amos showed his identity card to the bemused householder and decided to try the apologetic soft-soap approach first.

"I'm very sorry to trouble you, sir," Amos began, "but we're investigating the murder in this area of a man called Raymond Jones and I'd like to ask you a few questions."

"I'm afraid I can't help you, officer," the man said. "I've never heard of him. Or at least I hadn't until I heard about the murder."

He made to close the door. A more direct approach was needed.

"I'm afraid you <u>can</u> help us sir," Amos said. "In fact, it's vital you do. I believe that you do know Joanna Stevens, Mr Jones's neighbour. We are concerned for her safety."

The man looked startled. After a moment's hesitation he said uncertainly: "You'd better come inside."

However, it was Amos who was immediately back on the defensive as he had to ask the man his name. The fact that Amos obviously had little idea who he was talking to allowed his quarry to relax.

"My name is Gordon Brookes," he said with some amusement at Amos's discomfort. "Is there anything else about me you don't know?"

Just about everything, Amos thought to himself.

"You say you didn't know about Ray Jones," he said, "but can you rack your brains and think whether Miss Stevens has ever mentioned him. He was a client of hers."

Brookes shook his head.

"We never discussed business," he answered. "I have no interest whatsoever in accountancy or bookkeeping. Way beyond me."

"May I ask what you do?" Amos asked, pleased to get the conversation moving on inconsequential matters before building up to the crucial issues."

"I'm a postman," Brookes responded. "A humble postman."

Once again Amos was taken aback.

"Do you know Ken Clarke?" he asked.

"Of course I do," Brookes replied with a laugh. "You don't think he did it, do you? He's the last man on earth to commit a murder."

"No, no," Amos said hastily. "It's just that his wife Christine used to work for Mr Jones."

Brookes failed to respond and Amos decided that it was time he got down to the real point of his visit.

"How well do you know Miss Stevens?"

There was an awkward silence before Brookes finally responded.

"I've known Joanna since primary school."

"Are you two an item?"

"No."

"Is she romantically attached to anyone else to your knowledge?"

"I really don't feel any obligation to discuss Joanna's love life." Brookes said firmly. "Not that I'm saying she does or doesn't have one."

"Do you know of anyone who would like to be romantically linked to Miss Stevens?" Amos persisted. "Someone she has turned down and feels spurned?"

"The answer's still no," Brookes said, without indicating whether he meant no, there was no-one, or no, he wasn't prepared to comment on her love life.

"Did you ever go out with her?" Amos asked. "You were seen holding hands with her in the café."

"Is that a crime? So we held hands and now I want to kill her?

"Look, Joanna and I did go out briefly when we were teenagers but it never came to anything. She was way out of my league. We've stayed good friends ever since. I'm the one she turns to when she's feeling down and I'll always be there for her when she needs me but that's as far as it goes.

"And that, officer, is about as far as I can help you."

Amos was left feeling that all lines of inquiry were going down blind alleys. Yet he also felt that one of those alleys must be the right one. He resolved that, the following morning, he would pursue the one suspect who had had a guilty air about him from the moment the police had first set eyes on him.

Chapter 31

"Today, Sgt Swift," Amos announced perfunctorily, "we are going to do something we should have done sooner. Would you get the car please. We are going to obtain a warrant to search Jim Berry's house.

"We'll need a couple of constables from the team to take the place apart. It shouldn't take too long."

"Shall I get one of them to go for the warrant, Sir?" Swift asked.

"No, we'll get that ourselves. We can talk over the case as we go. Tell the other two to get round to Berry's and if he's there to keep him talking until we arrive."

Amos was keen to get the warrant himself because no progress had been made on his earlier order for one to be obtained immediately.

Swift drove and Amos talked, as much to himself, to put his own thoughts in order, as to his junior officer.

"It's all stacked against Berry. He's shifty, he looks guilty. He visited Killiney Court regularly. He knew the building. He had every reason to hate Jones. And he would be in the right flat. He must have known they had been renumbered.

"And yet it doesn't quite add up. Something's missing. He genuinely seems grateful to Jones and sees him as a saviour rather than a villain."

"He could have got access to Jones's flat though," Swift interjected. "If, as Berry says, Jones didn't want to be seen entertaining a scruffy down and out, he wouldn't have kept Berry on the doorstep. He'd have got him inside smartish before one of the neighbours saw him.

"Jones would be off guard. If Berry had finally rumbled him and come for revenge, Jones wouldn't have realised it."

Swift pulled into the drive of the magistrate who had been alerted to sign the paperwork. They were spotted from the house window and the door swung open as Amos raised his hand to the knocker.

The magistrate was a former school headmistress who had recently retired, a stern woman with a touch of humanity. She raised an eyebrow.

"I see you have turned up in person, inspector," she remarked dryly. "Should I take this as an honour?"

"It's always an honour to visit you, Miss Woodward," Amos remarked unabashed.

"Humph," she said, looking at the papers. "It's more to do with the importance of the Jones case than the pleasure of seeing me."

Woodward had a Bible waiting on the telephone table in the hall. She preferred not to allow the police too far into her home on these occasions, thus maintaining a division between law enforcement and judiciary.

Amos took the oath and gave Woodward a quick resume of the potential case against Berry. She signed the papers and Amos took them back without a word. His mind was still on the subject. In the car he picked up where he had left off.

"Let's consider who else there is. There's the women in Jones's life, perhaps a jilted lover. And Warren certainly had a motive. Jones had rumbled him. He'd left a message on the answering machine trying to fix up to see him. Suppose Jones relented and allowed him to pop round to plead his case. No one was likely to see Warren nip next door and back again.

"Foster's another with opportunity. He could wander around and no one would think anything of it. He would just be doing his job, sweeping the landings.

"He could have gained access to Jones's flat on a pretext. But what's his motive? Same with the security guard on duty that night. He had opportunity. We know from Foster he used to wander from his post for a cigarette. He could easily have slipped upstairs for a few minutes instead. Perhaps he's got some grudge against Jones from a past life.

"The trouble with them all, though, is how did Jones come to be murdered in his bed?"

"Could he have been hit somewhere else in the flat and then moved?" Swift suggested.

"Not with all that blood on the bed," Amos objected. "That's where he was killed."

"Then unless Jones had homosexual tendencies that we haven't uncovered yet, the murderer was a woman after all."

"Joanne Stevens," Amos mused. "Well, she was another with opportunity. Jones could have responded to her message on the answering machine and asked her down to talk over how they were going to deal with Warren. Then she lured him into bed."

"With an iron bar?" It was Swift's turn to raise an objection. "How did that get there?"

By now she was pulling up outside Berry's small and humble home. Amos jumped out and rapped on the door.

Two detective constables were already there, sent on ahead to keep Berry talking. Berry's joy at having the inquisition interrupted was short lived. The smile was quickly wiped from his face as he found Amos on his doorstep with Swift right behind him. Amos brushed passed the muttering Berry and was into the small front room before producing his precious piece of paper.

"It's a search warrant, Mr Berry," he announced briefly. "We are going to search your house."

Berry made no protest. He sat down in one of the two dilapidated armchairs that had been vacated by a detective constable when Amos had walked in. He said not a word.

"We'll start upstairs. You can accompany us if you wish," Amos offered.

Berry shook his head. Amos nodded to Swift to indicate that she was to stay with Berry. If he feared that the latter was about to remove some incriminating piece of evidence he need not have worried. Berry ignored Swift and sat motionless, staring at the threadbare carpet.

Up the narrow staircase with the walls painted lime green, the three male officers found two small bedrooms and a bathroom. One bedroom was empty. The bare floorboards were all firmly laid down and showed no signs of having been lifted. DC Cooke went into the bathroom and the other officer into the bedroom that Berry slept in.

Amos hovered at the top of the stairs where he could watch the search of both rooms. There was nothing of interest in the small wooden bathroom cabinet with a sliding glass front: just a shaving brush and razor together with a toothbrush that had seen better days. There was not even a tube of toothpaste.

The officer took a perfunctory peep into the toilet system.

Suddenly Amos commented: "Stand in front of the cabinet."

Startled, Cooke did as he was told.

"It's the only mirror in the bathroom," Amos went on. "There's no bulb in the socket. The window to your right is the only source of light. That's why Berry shaves better on that side of his face, Sherlock."

Amos mooched into the bedroom. The wallpaper was old and floral. Simple red curtains, heavy and faded, hung open. The matching carpet was well worn.

The bed was unmade and a pair of trousers and a shirt were lying on a wooden chair.

The constable had already been through the modest contents of a chest of drawers. Amos opened the door of a single wardrobe, the only other piece of furniture in the room. In the bottom were a pair of shoes with distinct traces of mud. Amos picked them up.

A pair of trousers had similar splashes around the turnups. Amos took possession of these items of clothing and left his constable to check through the rest.

"What exactly are we looking for?" The officer asked.

Amos shrugged.

"Anything that might link him to the murder. Who knows?"

Amos peered into the pale blue bathroom, with its dirty, uncurtained window to the right of the wash basin. Paint was peeling from the wall in places.

There were strips of black mould along part of the rubber sealing where the bath met the wall. The officer in here had unscrewed the side panel of the bath but had discovered nothing except dust and pipes.

Amos plodded downstairs, where he could hear Swift opening and closing drawers. He held the shoes in one plastic bag and the trousers in another. Berry opened his mouth to protest but Amos spoke first.

"I'm taking these in to have the mud analysed," he announced abruptly.

A few minutes later the two constables came down the stairs empty handed.

"Thanks for your cooperation, Mr Berry," Amos said with comical courtesy. "My sergeant will give you a receipt for the shoes and trousers.

"We'll be in touch."

Chapter 32

It was early evening when Amos went along to interview Jack and Vera Smith in flat 8D. There was no need to take another officer along. They were all working long enough hours as it was. Amos would add to the burden only when it was necessary.

Mrs Smith seemed a little annoyed at having to answer the door and somewhat more annoyed at seeing Amos's warrant card.

"I can't think why you want to talk to us again," she said peevishly. "We gave up half an hour to talk to your constable. It's hardly our fault if he didn't write it all down in the first place – not that we know anything about this business anyway," she added hastily.

Amos stood before the open door, taking the tirade in resigned silence while maintaining an air of expecting to be admitted. Unable to shake him off, Mrs Smith added with a pause: "Well, I suppose you'll have to come in then. But you'll have to wait. We're still eating. Mr Smith has been on the go all day and he likes his evening meal in peace."

Amos grunted assent and stepped inside. Mrs Smith showed him into the living room with a perfunctory "wait here" and disappeared into the kitchen/diner, closing the door behind her.

Amos was not too sorry for a few moments delay. It gave him time to put his thoughts in order after another dispiriting day. It also presented the opportunity to assess the Smiths by looking round their living room.

The furniture was modern and expensive, chrome and leather, designed to impress rather than for comfort. There was one older leather chair, sagging a little from usage. It was of the type that could be adjusted to lean back in with a footrest swinging up in front. Presumably Mr Smith liked his comfort when he was at home, whatever he might inflict on his wife and visitors.

There was a display cabinet and a television cabinet that was at this moment closed. Of books there was not a trace. Amos strolled across to the display cabinet and peered in. There was little on show, just a tea service spread thinly to fill the available space.

At this point the Smiths returned to the room.

"We used to have Mr Smith's tankard he was given when he switched jobs and his silver trophy when he was county surveyor of the year but they mysteriously disappeared," Mrs Smith said in a tone of voice that seemed to blame Amos personally for the losses.

"We keep the cabinet locked now. Still," she added as if graciously forgiving Amos for the outrage, "I don't suppose you came to talk about our missing items."

"No," Amos replied, "I came to talk about last Friday evening, the night Raymond Jones died."

"Like I said to you at the door, I can't understand why you want to talk to us. I told your constable earlier, we weren't here anyway."

"But I understand you were here, at least until late in the evening," Amos rejoined. "You were seen leaving these premises quite late."

"Well, yes," said Mrs Smith as one patiently explaining the obvious to a person of inferior intelligence. "But we had left long before Mr Jones died."

"You know what time Mr Jones was killed?" Amos blurted out with incredulity.

"Not exactly," Mrs Smith replied, her patience gradually evaporating. "Of course we don't know exactly when it happened. But it must have been during the night, surely, when everybody was certain to be asleep. It's obvious."

"What time did you leave?" Amos brought the conversation back from speculation to fact.

Mr Smith decided to take a grip. "It was about half past ten, or quarter to eleven. We generally travel at night to avoid the traffic. I came home early, had three hours sleep while Mrs Smith packed and we took the cases down in the lift. I can't tell you the precise time because I couldn't see my watch. We were just about to put the case into the boot when we had the power failure."

"Power failure?" Amos echoed in surprise.

"Power failure," Mrs Smith said firmly. "So you work out what time we left just by checking with the electricity people what time the power failed. We remarked how lucky we were to get to the bottom of the block before it happened. We would have had to carry the case all the way down from the top floor in the dark – or even worse we could have been trapped in the lift."

She shuddered visibly at the thought.

"You know about the power failure, of course."

Mrs Smith had no difficulty detecting Amos's discomfort.

"No-one has put a precise time on the power cut," the detective improvised.

"Hmmm," snorted Mrs Smith, unconvinced. "Anyway, we drove off to our daughter's in Bristol and didn't return until the Wednesday. She had rung us on the Thursday night because she was feeling poorly. Luckily my husband had a few days off owing to him from work so we got off as soon as we could.

"Daphne – our daughter – has a little boy and a new baby. So like I told you in the first place, we had long gone when Mr Jones was ..." she baulked at the cold word murder and finished, "... was killed."

"Did you see anybody at any point as you were taking things down to the car and leaving? Anyone from Killiney Court or a stranger?" Amos asked.

"No, as we told your constable, it was all quiet," Mrs Smith said. "Not a mouse was stirring – not that we have mice at Killiney Court," she added hastily.

"Please think carefully. You're quite sure you saw no-one?"

"I've told you already. We saw no-one apart from the security man in his little box."

"Did you see any unfamiliar vehicle parked under the block – or outside on the road?"

Again the answer was negative.

"Mr Smith, did you ever work for or with Mr Jones," Amos inquired innocently.

Mrs Smith looked fit to explode but her husband put his hand gently on her arm without even a glance at his wife.

Rather, he looked unflinchingly into Amos's eyes and replied coldly and steadily: "I have done some work for Raymond Jones in the distant past.

"I have a wife and daughter. If my wife was starving, I would have worked for him again. If my daughter was starving I would have worked for him again. But as I was able to feed them both, for my part I would rather have starved."

"Did you have any business dealings with Mr Jones?" Amos persisted. "On a business to business footing rather than personal."

Mr Smith looked at him suspiciously.

"Not particularly," he answered vaguely. "Of course, our company did work occasionally for one of Jones's companies or one of the companies that was in with him. You couldn't avoid it. If you worked in this county you couldn't avoid him altogether.

"But I never worked for him and I never had any direct business dealings with him," Smith concluded with some vehemence.

"Did you know him personally?" Amos persisted.

This time it was Mrs Smith who answered.

"Not particularly. We spoke if we saw him, of course."

This repetition of "of course" was beginning to annoy Amos.

Mrs Smith went on: "We didn't see him much. He didn't mix in our circle but we were civil, of course."

"Thank you for your time," Amos said, rising. "You're not likely to be disappearing for another weekend, are you? If you get another emergency call you'll let me know, of course."

Amos took the lift only as far as the third floor, the bottom one that had flats. He trotted down the stairs to Nick Foster's cubby hole of a home, which was not served by the lift, and knocked sharply on the door. Presently he could hear the lone occupant shuffling to the door.

"Who is it?" came the grumpy tones from within. "I'm off duty."

"Inspector Amos. I'm on duty."

"I've locked up."

"Just open the door," Amos said wearily. "I'm not coming in but I can't talk to you through a lump of wood."

The door opened immediately and without the aid of a key but it swung only six inches ajar. Nick Foster stuck his face into the gap.

"I can't open it any further," was the next excuse. "I've got boxes behind it. I'm sorting out my collection."

"Why didn't you tell me about the power cut?" Amos demanded. "Anyone could have been moving around in the dark."

"What power cut?"

"I have just been informed," Amos said firmly, "That there was a power failure on the Friday night that Ray Jones died. Just after half past ten. You never mentioned it."

"I never mentioned it because it's the first I've heard of it. I would have been in bed fast asleep but I'm surprised no one else told me about it. They usually come to me soon enough with their moans," Foster grumbled.

"They'd have had to reset their videos and electric clocks if the power went off. And their central heating timers. Hang on a minute."

Foster disappeared for a few moments then returned.

"The clock on my electric oven is still OK so the power can't have been off. I hate cooking with electric. We used to have gas when the council had the place."

Amos turned away puzzled, ignoring the end of Foster's rambling. It was a curious thing to make up if it was not true. Why would the Smiths invent such a silly lie? The inspector determined to make further inquiries next day.

But he was back at Killiney Court before he had chance to do so. An urgent call from an agitated Mrs Brown, the woman who first informed him of the petty thefts, was relayed to his home as he was eating an early breakfast.

Chapter 33

Amos rang Mrs Brown back as soon as he got the message. She was very excited and not entirely coherent.

"Mr Brown says you must come at once. He's standing guard and won't let anyone touch anything until you arrive. He's already stopped the dustbin men taking it away. There's all sorts. Please, inspector, you must come quickly. Mr Brown daren't even go to the toilet in case someone takes anything away while his back is turned."

Amos reckoned the best way to find out what the commotion was about would be to drive to Killiney Court right away rather than trying to interrogate his excitable informer.

He stuffed the bacon from off his plate between two slices of bread, wiped the grease from his fingers and slung on his jacket and coat, leaving the egg and baked beans to coagulate. He drove quickly along the still empty roads, eating his sandwich at the same time in defiance of the chief constable's road safety exhortations.

It was just gone 8 am when he reached the block of flats that were now becoming only too familiar to him. The same sentinel was on duty from last night, though not the one who had stood vigil in vain on the fateful Friday.

Mrs Brown hurried from under the block to greet him.

"Thank you, inspector, thank you," she puffed as she grasped his hand. "Here, round the back."

The two walked behind the lift shaft to where Mr Brown was standing triumphantly over a dozen or more cardboard and wooden boxes.

"They were here, this morning, waiting to be taken away by the dustbin men," he proclaimed. "It was sheer chance I spotted them. You see," he went on confidentially, "We put our rubbish into black sacks and drop them down a chute. Once a week the dustcart comes to take the bags away. They just open the doors at the bottom of the chutes.

"Well, I knew they would be coming this morning and we wanted to get rid of this old television set. It won't work and it's cheaper to buy a new one rather than get this repaired. So Mrs Brown and I carried it down. We're not supposed to have any extra rubbish but the men don't mind if you throw it on the cart yourself.

"That's when I found all these boxes. They were all taped up but I decided to have a look inside one. Now you remember we told you about the meeting we had with all the people in the block who had had things go missing? I immediately recognised some of the items in the box.

"So I opened another. Would you believe I actually found a couple of the things of ours that had vanished and we'd forgotten about.

"The dustbin men turned up at that moment but I stopped them from taking the boxes. They didn't need much persuading because they would have had to throw them onto the lorry themselves. In all the excitement we forgot to put our own TV on!"

Mr Brown looked ruefully at the useless electrical appliance still lying beside the sealed boxes.

Amos peeped inside the two opened boxes. There was no doubt where they had come from. They were the boxes that he had seen in Nick Foster's flat a few days earlier. No wonder Foster had not wanted him in the previous evening.

Perhaps the boxes really had been behind the door, stocked ready to be dumped early that morning.

Sgt Swift arrived at that moment.

"Sorry you beat me to it, Sir," she apologized unnecessarily. "I came as soon as HQ rang me but I got stuck at roadworks getting round Lincoln. The only piece of road in the entire county being resurfaced and I picked it."

"Ring Martin and get him down here with a couple of lads and a van. All this lot," he indicated with a sweep of his hand, "will have to be stored along with Jones's files. I want a list of every item. We'll have to get all the residents to identify their belongings but they can't have them back yet.

"You'll be called in due course," he added politely to the Browns, "but I hope you understand that this could be important evidence and we shall have to hold it for the time being."

Mr Brown nodded his assent.

"I'm being ungracious," Amos said suddenly. "I'm most grateful, Mr Brown," he added with a slight bow. "Well done."

The inspector thought for a moment then added: "By the way, do you know if there was a power cut on the Friday that Mr Jones died? It's probably nothing but it might just be important."

"Our electricity didn't go off," Mrs Brown replied quickly. "Not before we went to bed, anyway."

"Not after, either," Mr Brown added. "The clock on our video needs resetting if you unplug it. So if the power had failed the clock would have been flashing to be reset. What on earth made you think the electricity had gone off?"

"What indeed," replied Amos thoughtfully, and the Browns were too polite to press him further.

With Swift left in charge of the booty until it could be carted away, Amos went off in search of Foster. For once, the caretaker was not broom pushing or even broom leaning, his ear wagging for gossip.

Amos felt anxious. He took the steps two at a time to the mezzanine floor and rapped loudly on Foster's door. There was no response. Amos turned the handle. The door was unlocked and the officer entered. A quick search of the small flat revealed that all of Foster's "collections" had gone.

So, too, had Foster.

Chapter 34

Amos barked out an order to get a description of Foster to all officers.

"He can't have got far. He doesn't drive. Try the bus and train stations at Lincoln. We'd better alert Skegness and Boston. It's just possible he's got an early bus to pick up a train there. Skegness is our better bet. He doesn't need to change buses and he gets further away from here faster but it backs him into a corner."

Amos remained alone to make a cursory search of the flat. There was not a single photograph of the missing man. He led a lonely existence with not even his own image for company. No wonder he spent so much time under the block, sweeping away and scrounging a little human contact. It would drive me crackers, Amos thought.

In a drawer was an address book. The inside front cover was inscribed in a child's handwriting: "To Uncle Nick, from Chloe."

The same handwriting had supplied a family name and address in Wakefield under the letter D. A couple more names and telephone numbers had been added, presumably by Foster, but that was the sum total of his recorded acquaintances.

Amos went down to the car park guard. It seemed that Foster had fled when Mr Brown discovered the packages waiting for the dustbin men. He could not, therefore, have got far.

The inspector drove straight to Horncastle market square, a meeting point of local bus routes between Lincoln, Skegness, Louth and Boston.

Most of the railway lines in the county had been ripped up some 30 years past. Realistically, the one from Skegness through Boston to Sleaford and Grantham, with connections to London, Nottingham and Doncaster was Foster's best bet if he intended using that form of transport. The alternative was by taking a bus to Lincoln.

A travel agent had set up shop on the opposite side of the rutted tarmac where the buses turned, operating also as an office for a local bus company that ran a daily morning service to London.

The woman behind the desk was quite certain that no-one of Nick Foster's description had taken the service that morning, although the bus had been quite full. Amos did a mental calculation. It was unlikely, though just possible, that Foster had had time to catch it.

An inspector from the Lincolnshire Road Car Company who was timing buses in and out of the town was his only other hope of a positive sighting. This proved even less satisfactory: the inspector did not remember anyone resembling Foster travelling alone. However, his concern was to check that the buses were on time, not to imprint on his brain images of all the passengers.

It was vital to find Foster for two reasons. Firstly, he was a major suspect in the murder of Raymond Jones. He had had ample opportunity, although there was no obvious motive. Secondly, if he was not the murderer he could just possibly hold a vital clue without realising it. Foster had been safe in Killiney Court with the heavy police presence. He was vulnerable out in the wide open world.

Amos returned to the murder inquiry room set up in the town's police station and surveyed the evidence mounted on boards. It led nowhere. He took Foster's thin address book and rang the Wakefield number. A woman answered.

"I'm sorry to trouble you," Amos began, "and please don't be alarmed but this is the Lincolnshire police. We need to get in touch with a Mr Nick Foster who has apparently gone away for a short break. I wondered if he had by any chance come to you."

"Good Lord, no," the woman replied. "Nick never went anywhere. The last time we saw him was a couple of Christmases ago. Even then my husband had to fetch him and he only stayed four days, thank goodness. He's my brother, by the way. He's all right but a little goes a long way. It's hard work trying to have a conversation with him."

Then suddenly, almost as an afterthought, the voice asked: "He's not in any kind of trouble, is he?"

"No, no," Amos replied soothingly though untruthfully. "Just something that's cropped up at the block of flats where he is the caretaker. He might be able to help. Please contact me immediately if by any chance he turns up."

Amos supplied his name and phone number.

Clearly news of the killing had not travelled to Yorkshire. It had not caught the media's imagination with a "Killiney Court Killing" or "Iron Bar Butcher" label. There was no knowing which murders would make national headlines. It was just the luck of the draw.

Amos tried the other two numbers in the underutilised address book. Neither call produced an answer. That was hardly surprising. By now, the occupants could well be at work or out shopping.

He rang the county police headquarters of the two areas where the addresses were located, supplied the name, address and telephone number in each case and asked for the occupant to be tracked down to find out if Foster had ever visited them.

He needed to know urgently if Foster turned up, no matter what time of day or night.

It was a pretty thin hope. In fact, it would be the following day before there was any further news of Foster.

Chapter 35

The first chill blast of autumn spread insidiously across the market place that afternoon. Constable John Lowe pulled together his jacket and cursed himself for risking venturing out without at least a macintosh. Lowe, now in his mid-twenties, had never quite got used to the dry cold winds of the East coast in his seven years among the wolds and fens.

He came from the damper, sheltered valleys of Lancashire, moving eastwards when his father, long left idle by the demise of the cotton trade that once thrived in the moist atmosphere of the western Pennines, had decided to try his luck at the Butlins holiday camp near Ingoldmells. The establishment north of Skegness had happy holiday associations for the family and Lowe senior had reckoned that seasonal work was better than non-existent employment.

PC Lowe was under no illusions that there were icier days ahead and many of them. Siberia had not yet shed its summer heat, Lowe thought. Soon that cutting knife would slice across a Continent and a half, directed straight at Lincolnshire.

A little dust and a couple of chip papers snaked across the road. Little else stirred. It was half day closing and the town was, unusually, practically deserted. Lowe pulled into a doorway to escape the bite. There was no respite from that wind.

About 50 yards on was a small car that had trundled down the high street, pulled across the deserted market place and slipped into one of the marked bays. The occupant sat there for a minute or two, apparently reluctant to brave the elements. Finally the driver got out and strolled across the road to look in a shop window. It was a woman.

Lowe could never understand why some people seemed to enjoy looking at goods they had no intention of buying – indeed on this occasion the unknown female could not have bought even if she wanted to as the shop, like those on either side of it, was shut for the rest of the day.

She did not turn around as a man in his fifties approached her. The male figure came out of the pawnshop, one establishment that was open, on the far side from Lowe and his face was visible full on. Lowe knew him immediately. He was the father of one of the boys who had been in Lowe's class at senior school.

Then Lowe remembered who the woman was as well. She was Elsie Norman, one of the neighbours of the man who was murdered. He had interviewed her.

Norman turned sharply as the man stopped next to her. Lowe could see them clearly although he was looking through the side pane of the doorway and out through the front plate glass window of the premises where he stood out of sight of the other two. It was only now, though, as Norman swung her back to him, that the officer could see a small package under the woman's arm.

The man was scruffily dressed and had clearly fallen onto harder times since Lowe's school days. Was he about to mug the woman, Lowe wondered. It certainly looked like it, for the man reached out towards the package and Norman pulled back instinctively.

There was no problem. Lowe could easily outrun the thief. The two figures down the street were engaged in animated conversation for a few moments. Out of the corner of his eye, Lowe spotted another lone pedestrian walking down the street on the opposite side but heading in the direction of the two figures he had under surveillance.

Norman had spotted the newcomer, too. To Lowe's surprise, Norman thrust the package into the man's welcoming arms and scurried back to her car. Within seconds she had opened the door, slipped inside, fastened her seat belt and started up. Quickly she backed out of the space and pulled away from the parking area before disappearing smoothly down the narrow road at the far end away from Lowe.

The man stuck the package under his coat and set off walking up the street towards the constable. Lowe slipped out about 10 yards in front of the source of his curiosity. The man was startled and almost stopped but he decided to try to keep going.

"Hello," said Lowe pleasantly. "It's Jim Berry isn't it? Do you remember me? John Lowe. I was in the same class as your Brian."

"Yes, yes, of course," Berry muttered, pushing the package more firmly down the inside of his coat so it was completely out of sight.

"Found a shop open?" Lowe asked mischievously, pointing to the slight bulge in Berry's jacket. Berry looked a little startled.

"Just a box of chocolates," he lied. "The sweet shop down at the end is open."

Lowe hesitated. He had no grounds for demanding that Berry should produce the package. In any case, Berry was now hurrying off in the direction of the village where he lived, though it would be a long walk. However, Lowe determined to relate the incident to Amos, since it involved a resident of Killiney Court.

The uniformed constable did not realise that it also involved a key suspect in Jim Berry and was to be quite astonished at the chief inspector's enthusiastic response to this titbit.

Chapter 36

Foster sat once again in the interview room at Horncastle police station. He accepted his lot with an air of resignation.

A uniformed officer was recounting breathlessly what had been for him his first exhilarating experience since joining the force.

"We got a call from Skegness first thing this morning, Sir," he related to Amos, who was seated opposite Foster.

"They weren't sure it was Foster but he matched the description and he was travelling alone. He caught an early train to Nottingham. We shot down the A15 and intercepted the train at Heckington. Foster didn't try to deny who he was and he came quietly enough."

Amos thanked the officer for his sterling work and nodded towards the door. The young man was patently disappointed not to be allowed to stay for the interrogation of his capture.

"So you laid low in Skeggy for the night," Amos remarked with a disarming smile. "And now you're going to go back to your work as if nothing much has happened."

Foster gasped.

"You're … you're not going to …" he started before falling abruptly silent.

"I shall drop you at the nearest bus stop to Killiney Court. You will walk back to the building and tell anyone who asks that you had to rush off because of a family bereavement. Do you think you can manage that convincingly?"

Foster nodded.

"Then you will make your way up to your rooms and stay there until I am ready to interview you about your various misdemeanours. Don't cause me any more trouble."

Foster again nodded his assent.

After leaving the caretaker at the appointed spot, Amos arrived unannounced at Joanna Stevens' office, to the surprise of the officer on duty, who was yawning in the corner, and Stevens herself.

"This is a great honour, inspector," she said with heavy sarcasm.

The magistrate had said something similar when he applied for the search warrant for Jim Berry's house. Was he really so aloof?

Amos addressed himself to the officer first. The startled constable was already on his feet, embarrassed at being caught almost napping.

"I'll take over now," Amos said with a sharp edged to his voice. "As you're near the end of your shift you can go straight home. They know at the station."

The officer gabbled his thanks, grabbed his waterproof jacket and scarpered.

"I suppose you send the most boring officers because you can most easily spare them," Stevens commented, but at least now there was a touch of amusement in her voice.

"Miss Stevens, would it be fair to say that you objected to having a police bodyguard in the first place?"

"You know perfectly well I did."

"And can I take it from your remarks that you have become no more enthusiastic about the arrangement?"

Stevens leaned forwards slightly, her interest awakened.

"You take it correctly," she said.

"You understand, Miss Stevens, that if I withdraw the police guard you must accept the entire responsibility for the decision?"

"Fine by me," Stephens said with growing keenness.

"The police presence is now withdrawn," Amos told her.

For the first time, he saw Stevens smile. It was a full, beautiful unguarded smile that took five, perhaps ten, years off her face. It was the first and last time Amos ever saw that smile.

Amos drove back to the murder headquarters. Having primed the officers whose help he would need, the inspector drove home and enjoyed a long soak in the bath.

He would have a light meal and an early night. He needed a full day to put his plan into action and tomorrow was his best chance.

Fingers crossed.

Chapter 37

Sir Robert Fletcher, Chief Constable of Lincolnshire, called Amos into his office early the following day.

"So how's the inquiry going into what's his name's murder?" Fletcher asked. "You know, that chap …what was his name?"

Amos knew well enough. There was just one murder inquiry proceeding in the entire county at that time so it was not hard to remember it, or the name of the victim.

"Jones, sir," Amos replied slightly stiffly.

He was not greatly anxious to get into a long, involved discussion on the subject. He did not want to have to tell his superior officer that there was no-one to arrest, no clear leads, no real developments to report, that it was not even clear that Jones was meant to be murdered.

Amos did have some thoughts about how he intended to develop the investigation but he did not want to discuss them with the head of the force.

"Jones, yes, Jones," Fletcher repeated rather non-committally. "Jones."

There was a silence as the Chief Constable mulled over some papers on his desk. Amos, able to avoid Fletcher's eye, shrugged and merely said: "Hmmmm."

Fletcher took out a pen and made a couple of amendments to the typed text in front of him. He always dealt in matters in strict order of priority. Finally he looked up.

"Well?" he asked. "Where are we up to with – what did you say he was called? – Jones?"

"We've had to interview a lot of people, sir," Amos replied. It sounded like a lame excuse. "Jones knew hundreds of people. We're sifting through the evidence now to see if we can find any specific lead."

Amos shut up. The more he said, the worse it sounded.

"What about that chap Berry?" asked the Chief Constable, who found it easier to remember the names of suspects rather than victims, especially when he was paying attention. "Yes, Berry."

"We can't touch him, sir. Absolutely no motive. He clearly wanted Jones alive and there is no suggestion that he knew Joanna Stevens or had any reason to break into her flat either."

Fletcher's mind was wandering back to the more important issue on the desk in front of him.

"I'm just off to Nottingham," he remarked.

It was the quarterly meeting of the chief constables of the East Midlands region. It was held in each county town in rotation and it was Nottingham's turn to entertain. They would be ringing up from the gate in a few moments to say that the chauffeur driven car was waiting.

Amos knew about the meeting. Everyone did. Fletcher had been going on about it for days to anyone whose ear he could bend.

"Ah, David," he called over Amos's shoulder to a young man hovering just inside the doorway. "Have you got the press release ready?"

Amos declined to turn to acknowledge the nervous and acne-inflicted youth who obediently ran the press office and who now bustled into the room. He handed Fletcher a piece of paper.

"We're going to discuss our strategy for a four-county blitz on drunk drivers this Christmas," Fletcher explained confidentially to Amos. "We've been the pioneers of random breath tests, a crusade to stamp out drink driving. I want to make sure there is no backsliding this time."

"How are the statistics bearing up?" Amos asked dryly. He realised his mistake even as the words slipped from his lips.

The more people who were stopped and breathalysed at random, the lower the percentage who were found to be actually over the limit.

Amos had, on more than one occasion, vented his frustrations at being given insufficient resources for crime fighting by making oblique reference to the frightening level of deaths and injuries on the roads of Lincolnshire, a toll apparently unstemmed by indiscriminate breath tests.

He always regretted speaking out of turn on the issue and this was certainly not the right time to be attracting the attentions of the Chief Constable. Amos desperately needed a free hand to pursue the gamble he had in motion.

Fletcher spluttered and waved out his press officer. The fury rose up over his face as David scrabbled together his papers, turned, dropped a sheaf, bent to pick it up and spilt more papers, then scrabbled them together once more and backed out of the room as if humbly leaving the presence of an oriental king.

The Chief Constable built himself up in the few seconds it took the hapless scribe to clear the doorway. Those few seconds were, however, long enough for him to recover his composure.

"More people are killed on our roads than in murders," he began. "Thirty times as many. More people are seriously injured than in grievous bodily harm cases. More are hurt than in common assaults. More financial loss is incurred in crashes than in muggings and burglaries. The human and economic cost of careless driving far outweighs the deliberate crimes committed every day.

"However, if you consider I am spending too much time cutting the carnage on our roads," he said in angry but controlled tones, "then I will oblige you. I will return to the office from Nottingham this evening and you can give me a full briefing on the Jones murder inquiry, including the list of suspects, the evidence you have gathered against them and the steps you propose to take to bring a speedy end to this inquiry. Then we will consider if I need to put a more experienced officer in charge."

Amos made to reply but the Chief Constable waved his unspoken words away airily.

"No, no, there's no need to submit your report in writing. I know how much you scorn red tape. You can tell me in person.

"Shall we say 7pm? That should give me adequate time to conduct the important business at the conference and get back here. I shall be delaying a dinner appointment to give you my valuable time so it had better be good."

Amos slid his hands behind his back and, unseen, dug his nails hard into the palms of his hands. Best to say no more. He had done enough damage. There were a few seconds of awkward silence as the Chief Constable returned behind his desk and stood there, the rich colour perceptively fading from his cheeks.

"Well, get along, Amos," he said in a tone that successfully combined mocking with sounding patronising. Fletcher walked over to the open door and held the handle in a false gesture of courtesy.

Amos shuffled away, head bowed.

Chapter 38

There were just three reporters and a photographer at the press conference that Amos hastily called for 12 noon, after he was satisfied that the Chief Constable was safely out of the way. Radio Lincolnshire, the Lincolnshire Echo and the local weekly were the sum total of interest in a routine murder inquiry lacking the salacious or the sensational angle that attracted the national press.

That suited Amos fine. No doubt the reporter from the local paper would try to earn a few pounds by selling what Amos had to say to the nationals but in any case nothing would appear there until the next day, if at all.

What Amos wanted was widespread publicity locally as quickly as possible. Time was very tight.

Amos spoke carefully and non-committally to the four stalwarts as they waited to make a formal start. At five past 12 Swift, the only other police officer present, said: "I don't think anyone else is coming, sir. We might as well start now."

It should have been the force's press officer organising the conference, Amos knew full well, but that would have meant the Chief Constable finding out and demanding to know what was to be said. Better to let him discover what was going on in due course, preferably when Amos was out of the office and unobtainable for as long as possible to allow the inevitable hue and cry to die down.

The photographer was a woman, still quite a rarity these days, Amos thought to himself as he took his place. She took a few shots of him sitting at a desk in front of the almost empty rows of chairs. Swift stood against the left hand wall near the door.

"Thank you for coming," Amos began in a somewhat apologetic tone of voice. "I have to tell you that the inquiry into the murder of the businessman Raymond Jones has come to a dead end."

Amos stumbled as he realised the bad taste of the unintended pun. Swift was startled. She had never seen Amos so ill at ease. Normally he exuded confidence, at least in public, no matter how unforthcoming an investigation was.

There was an audible gasp from the journalists, few though they were in number. One of them half stood up to ask a question but Amos recovered his composure and continued as the reporter sank back into his seat.

"I have to be realistic. There is no new evidence, nor are there any fresh leads. We do not have any genuine suspect with a real motive for killing Mr Jones. However, we are satisfied that there is no further danger to any residents in Killiney Court.

"The file will stay open, of course, but only two officers will officially remain on a case that is, frankly, going nowhere. Detective Sergeant Swift" – here Amos indicated the only other officer in the room with a short sweep of his left hand – "will continue in charge of the day-to-day conduct of the inquiry. She will be assisted by a detective constable. They will follow up any further information that comes in. I shall remain nominally in overall charge of the investigation and will again take control should circumstances require it."

Amos had taken the precaution of warning Swift what was coming. She stood impassively at her post.

The middle-aged man from the Echo half turned.

"How do you feel about this?" he asked Swift, ignoring Amos for the moment. "How many murder inquiries have you been on? Have you ever headed one before? What do you propose to do next?"

It was, however, Amos who answered.

"Detective Sergeant Swift is a very experienced and reliable officer who has been on various major investigations, including murder, with me and is perfectly capable of running an inquiry which, as I indicated, is inevitably going to be low key.

"I also mentioned that she can turn to me for assistance and advice if and when required. I prefer not to give details of any further steps Detective Sergeant Swift may take."

Amos was now back in control, speaking with an air of authority that discouraged further questions along those lines.

It was the young woman from the local radio station who asked the crucial question. She had the microphone to her tape recorder on the desk in front of Amos so she was not interested in what Swift might have to say.

"What about Joanna Stevens?" she asked sweetly. "Wasn't she supposed to be in danger? What about her police protection?"

"The police protection for residents of Killiney Court has been withdrawn," Amos said simply. Far from being put out by the bluntness of this question, which carried more than a hint of accusation, Amos looked quite content to hear it posed.

"What does Miss Stevens think about that?" the third reporter butted in.

"She entirely understands our reasons and is quite comfortable with the decision," Amos replied smoothly.

The reporters looked at each other slightly nonplussed. There really was little more they could think of to ask. They had come expecting to hear of a major breakthrough and here was Amos coldly calling the whole thing off.

The reporter from the Lincolnshire Echo suddenly looked at his watch, slipped his notebook into his jacket pocket and dashed off with the photographer. Unwilling to be scooped, the Lincolnshire Radio representative grabbed together her equipment, stuffed it quickly into her bag and gave chase.

Only the weekly newspaper reporter took his time. He looked at the figure of Amos leaning heavily on the desk, found nothing more to say, then walked unhurriedly past Swift and out of the door.

Amos glanced up at his junior officer.

"It could have been worse," he said with a sigh of relief. "It could have been much worse."

Chapter 39

It was mid afternoon and all was quiet as Amos pulled into Killiney Road.

"Glance up at the windows as we turn into Killiney Court," he told Swift. "See if you can spot anyone looking out."

The guard did not recognise the car as it pulled into the drive so the barrier stayed firmly down as he got out of his box to investigate.

"That's good, I suppose," Amos remarked. "We're not easily recognisable."

He had deliberately used a different, unmarked car from his earlier visits to the block.

Amos waited until the guard was almost alongside the driver's door before he slowly wound down the window. He wanted to spin it out slightly so it looked as if it was an ordinary visitor coming in.

"Oh, I beg your pardon, officer," the guard blurted out. "Sorry, I didn't recognise the car."

"That's all right," replied Amos pleasantly. "Just give me the visitors' book to sign. Then we're going to park up the back out of the way. Put the barrier down behind us and walk across to us casually. I want a quiet word."

"It's a bit awkward," the sentry stammered, looking round wildly for an excuse to refuse. "I'm not supposed to leave the post."

"Doesn't stop you from wandering round the back, does it?" Amos responded coldly as he started to wind up the window. "See you in a few moments."

The two stared at each other through the now raised pane of glass like two cats trying to outstare each other. The guard broke first.

As Amos drove down the side of the block, Swift reported: "There was no-one at any of the windows except that Norman woman. I had time to look at all of them while you were talking to the guard. Of course," she added hastily, "someone could have been watching from further back in the room where I wouldn't see them."

"That will have to do," Amos replied. "We're not dealing with certainties, just giving ourselves the best chance."

By now Amos had parked in Ray Jones's slot and the three occupants were getting out of the car.

"Next stop Nick Foster. You two wander up and engage him in idle chitchat for a couple of minutes. He's not down here so I assume he is in his room."

Swift and Martin set off up the stairs to the mezzanine floor. The guard peered through the back window of his box, saw Amos nod, slid uncertainly out of his shell and approached the police officer.

Amos looked at the floor and drew patterns with the toe of his shoe in the dust that accumulated unremittingly despite Foster's best endeavours. He did not look up until the guard was alongside him.

At last Amos looked him straight in the eye. "I want to keep my job and you want to keep yours," the chief inspector remarked simply.

The guard said nothing. It was his turn to stare at the floor.

"You will go back to your post and wait there. Operate the barrier as usual if anyone wants to come in or out. You will do nothing that arouses suspicion. In a few minutes Nick Foster will come down and speak to you. When he does so, you will leave the barrier up, walk round to the back of the lifts and stay there until we give you the all clear. Then you go back to your post and carry on as normal. Understand?

"It's not for me to report you to your employers," Amos added. "Not unless I feel vindictive."

"Thanks," said the guard with relief and gratitude in equal measures.

"Back to your post," bade Amos.

The guard went with measured stride. He did not look back. Amos was up the stairs two at a time. He found Martin standing lazily in the doorway of the caretaker's office, blocking Foster's exit.

Amos peered past Martin and saw Foster sitting at his little desk. Swift, hidden from view in the cramped space, could be heard going over Foster's story again. Foster looked relaxed. He had gone over his version of events of the murder weekend often enough to have it off pat.

A look of agitation crossed his face, however, when he glanced up and saw the senior of the three officers. Martin, unaware until then that Amos had come up swiftly and silently behind him, saw the changed look on Foster's face and stepped aside.

Amos nodded to Swift, whom he could now see and who broke off from the half-hearted interrogation and slid past him out of the room. Amos stepped neatly inside and closed the door behind him.

"I don't have time to mess about," he said briskly. "I want the set of keys you have to all the flats."

Foster was visibly taken aback. "What do you mean? What keys? All the residents have their own."

"But you keep a set from the days when this block belonged to the council. Are you going to hand them over or do I have to take them?"

Foster stood up and turned away.

"Where do you think you're going?" Amos demanded sharply.

"For the keys," Foster replied simply. "They're hidden in my bedroom."

Thank goodness, Amos thought to himself, Foster didn't try to call my bluff. Getting a search warrant would have left the inspector too tight for time.

"You don't normally keep them in your bedroom, do you? Where are they normally kept?"

By way of answer, the caretaker pulled open the top right hand drawer of the desk then closed it again.

Foster pushed back his chair and squeezed out from behind the desk. A door to his right led through into the tiny rooms that formed his modest living quarters. A few moments later he returned dangling the precious keys from one hand. It was a heavy bunch held together on a length of grubby string.

Amos had taken a plastic bag out of his pocket and indicated to Foster to drop the keys into it. It might be vital to know if there were any prints on them other than Foster's. Amos slipped the bulky bag into his pocket with some difficulty. It left quite a bulge.

"Thank you," he said, "for this evidence."

The accent was on the word evidence. The officer was trying not to betray the haste with which he needed to move. He didn't want Foster dragging his feet on purpose.

Amos continued: "Now you will take your brush and mess about near the bottom of the stairs. When my constable comes to the landing and signals to you, you will tell the sentry to leave the barrier up and to go round the back for a smoke. Tell him those are my orders."

Then the next bit deliberately: "You will go round the back with him and stay out of sight. Neither you nor the guard will tell anyone we have been here this afternoon. Is that all clear?"

Foster grunted grudgingly. Amos left the room satisfied that the caretaker would follow his instructions.

"This way," the inspector said to his two accomplices. "One more visit."

Chapter 40

Swift and Martin glanced at each other but neither guessed where they were going. Amos led them up to the first floor of flats, now numbered level three, and pressed the lift button. They could hear the lift whirr into action.

When the doors opened Amos was inside in a trice and pressed a button even before Swift or Martin could see which one. Martin, the last one in, was almost caught by the closing doors. The sensors picked up his movement and the doors opened again.

Amos stabbed the "close doors" button two or three times impatiently. There was no immediate response. Then suddenly the doors jerked and started to close. All three officers watched the strip of numbers over the lift door that indicated which floor they were at.

As the lift moved up, 3 went dead, then 4, the floor where Joanne Stevens lived, lit up. This was not, however, their destination for the lift continued to rise: 4 went out and 5 came to life.

This time the lift did stop. Amos stepped out and purposefully headed for flat 5A. He rapped sharply on the door, following this with a ring on the door bell. There was silence.

Elsie Norman, they knew, had seen them come in and clearly did not wish to receive them.

"Open the letterbox, Martin, and tell her we saw her at the window," Amos ordered wearily. Martin bent forward and did as he was asked.

Amos's patience snapped and, bending to the letterbox himself, added coldly: "Do you want us back with a search warrant?"

That did the trick, for Norman was immediately heard bustling up to the door. The clink of the chain being undone could be heard clearly and Norman pulled the door a couple of inches ajar.

Amos had his right hand on it, pushing Norman back until the gap was wide enough to slide through. He advanced on the helpless woman, forcing her to retreat so that the other two officers could gain admittance.

"Shut the door behind you," he instructed Martin curtly.

Norman was giving no more ground than she could help.

"What's the fuss?" she asked cantankerously. "I was coming. I was just in the kitchen making a cup of tea."

"Nice of you to offer," Amos remarked sardonically, "but we've no time for a brew."

Then he turned deadly serious: "Elsie Norman, I am arresting you in connection with the murder of Raymond Jones."

Norman stared at Amos in silence for a few seconds before letting out a low gasp. Then, recovering from the momentary shock, she laughed mockingly into his face.

Amos could not return her stare. He turned away to the window and looked out.

"Read her the caution," he ordered the constable without turning.

Martin supplied the necessary words but Norman was becoming increasingly truculent.

"You haven't got anything on me," she exclaimed scornfully. "Are you seriously arresting me? Come on then, let's get down to the police station. We'll see how long you can hold me."

Amos glanced down at the chair and table near the window. A pair of knitting needles held three badly knitted rows. Progress seemed to be rather slow considering the amount of time she apparently devoted to the task.

Perhaps she spent all her time admiring the view. She could certainly see some way, into the entrances to buildings on either side of Killiney Court and those across the road.

Amos suddenly strode past Norman and flung open a bedroom door. He had moved to a second door before Norman had a chance to move or call out.

This room was in darkness except for the glow of a dim red bulb. Norman leapt at Amos, preventing him from opening the door more than a few inches. She slammed the door shut.

"What do you think you're doing, poking round my flat?" she demanded angrily. "Have you got a search warrant? Well, have you?"

Instead of replying, Amos sent Martin off to remove Foster and the guard. Amos, Norman and Swift waited in silence until Martin returned to give the all clear.

"Let's move quickly," Amos said to Norman. "I don't suppose you want to be seen being taken away by police officers."

The small party quickly entered the lift and made their way to the ground floor. There was no-one around as they slipped into the waiting car and nipped out through the open barrier.

Chapter 41

Amos knew it was too much to hope that his luck would last all day. The Chief Constable was back sooner than anyone expected, the Nottingham meeting having found the four leaders in general agreement. To make matters worse, he had been listening to Radio Lincolnshire on the car radio on his way back to headquarters.

The sensational news about the murder inquiry was, not surprisingly, the lead item in the local news bulletin, pushing the collapsing price of pork and its disastrous consequences for local pig breeders into second place.

Fortunately Fletcher was chauffeur-driven or he would have become one of the accident victims that caused him so much anguish. He stormed into the building, shouting for the wretched press officer as he came.

Poor David had been dreading this moment since the Lincolnshire Echo had arrived half an hour earlier and he had seen the front page lead. He had taken the evening newspaper into Fletcher's office half a dozen times, putting it on his desk, turning it round, straightening it, picking it up and taking it out again.

David met Fletcher in the corridor. The Chief Constable wrenched the paper from the press officer's paralysed hands and marched without a pause into his office, reading the headline as he went. It confirmed the outrageous radio report.

Fletcher slammed the paper down on his desk.

"Where have they got all this from?" he demanded.

"I ... I d-don't know," stammered the quaking David.

"They can't both have made it up," snapped Fletcher. "Where's Amos."

"He's been out all afternoon, Sir," David blurted out. "I've been trying to get hold of him."

"Ah, here's Swift," the Chief Constable interrupted. "Perhaps she can enlighten us."

Swift had indeed been entrusted by Amos to head off wrath and interference. She smiled sweetly at Fletcher.

"Oh, good, you're back, Sir," she remarked as if previously unaware that the officer had returned from Nottingham. "I was just coming in to brief David but I can give you the good news first hand.

"We have made an arrest in the Ray Jones case. Amos is interviewing her now and we should have everything wrapped up by tomorrow morning when she will appear in court. There's tons of evidence in her flat and we expect to have a full confession when she is confronted with it. There'll be no point in denying what she has been up to."

"She?" asked Fletcher, taken by surprise at this unexpected but favourable turn of events.

"One of the women in the flats. Amos said to assure you he will fully update you personally as soon as he can. He can't break off at the moment as he is at a crucial stage in the interview," she added hastily.

Chapter 42

It was Amos who nearly gave the game away. The constant, intense pressure of the past few days, the lack of sleep, had finally caught up with him. Lulled by the boredom of waiting in the dark, unable to do or say anything, he dosed fitfully. A couple of times Swift had nudged him firmly but gently as he built up to a snore. Each time Amos awoke with a start then settled back again.

No-one spoke.

The clink of metal brought him in from his reverie. Half asleep, he grunted instinctively and shifted uneasily. There was silence. For a few seconds he wondered if he had scared off his quarry with his involuntary noise.

Amos was soon reassured. A somnolent sound in the dead of night was hardly untoward. There was another click as the front door was pushed, only for the chain to pull taut.

The inspector had hesitated over putting the chain on. It represented an obstacle to the intruder, who might panic and flee. Yet surely this simple precaution would be expected. It could have raised suspicion to leave the chain off.

There were more indeterminate and very quiet noises. With luck, someone was levering out the end of the chain from the door jamb.

"Come on," Amos urged silently. "Don't back off."

Silence returned but now Amos was alert, striving to hear any movement. There was nothing.

Then suddenly came the sound of frenzied blows crashing down on the bed accompanied by the grunts of the assailant. The unseen stranger paused, panting a little. Then there was silence again.

Amos gripped Swift's arm in case she moved precipitously. "The light," he willed the stranger. "Switch the light on."

Nothing happened. Yet Amos knew the intruder was still there, breathing heavily with the exertion but gradually more steadily, hardly daring to switch the light on after the previous disaster of breaking into the wrong flat and killing the wrong person.

Finally came the sound of someone feeling around and catching things in the dark. An ornament crashed to the floor and shattered, making Swift jump. Amos gripped her arm more tightly.

Suddenly the bedside light was on.

Amos stepped forward and opened the wardrobe door that he had hidden behind. Swift stood looking apprehensively over his shoulder. Before them stood the dismayed figure of Jim Berry.

Berry remained motionless, stunned for a few seconds. His eyes went from police officers to the bed. There was no tell-tale patch of oozing blood.

He looked back at Amos, then at the bar now lying where he had dropped it half way down the bed.

"Don't bother," said Amos quietly. "There are too many of us."

Martin appeared through the front door of the apartment even as he spoke. Two of the larger members of the uniformed branch followed him.

Berry grabbed the sheets in fury and yanked them back ferociously. Beneath them sat a row of cushions. A wig lay on the pillow, now only partly covering the crushed remains of a dummy's head.

"Oh dear," said Amos coldly. "I shall have to buy the hairdressing salon a new one."

Then turning to Martin, he said: "Give him the caution."

Berry was not listening. He was transfixed by the ludicrous sight of the shattered inanimate objects on the bed.

"You understand?" Amos asked when Berry failed to respond to the caution. There was no response.

"Do you understand?" Amos asked in a louder tone.

Berry nodded, though Amos doubted whether he had taken in what Martin had said, or even quite taken in that he had been tricked.

"You should have let me kill her," he said sadly. "She was evil."

Berry used the past tense, Amos noticed, perhaps still not accepting that he had failed for the second time to rid himself and the world of Elsie Norman.

Chapter 43

"So how do we stand?" the chief constable demanded when Amos arrived at headquarters next morning. "Are you in a position to charge Elsie Norman?"

"Yes," Amos replied simply.

"Has she admitted killing Raymond Jones? How much evidence have you got against her to make a murder charge stick?"

Amos had had no more than four hours sleep, having escorted Berry back to the cells, and was enjoying the pleasure of winding up the Chief Constable, safe in the knowledge that a successful conclusion to the case, plucked almost out of thin air, would afford him adequate protection.

"Norman has certainly not admitted to killing Jones, nor did I ever expect her to. On the contrary, she continues to deny it emphatically, as I discovered when I spoke to her half an hour ago."

"But," the Chief Constable spluttered, "but David has just passed to me a draft press release saying you made an arrest yesterday and the suspect would be appearing in court this morning. In fact," he continued, getting hot under the collar, "when I challenged Swift last night she told me you had arrested Norman for the murder."

"I'm afraid that was a little white lie, sir," Amos interrupted with the air of a penitent, "to buy me time to catch the real killer. The murderer has indeed been arrested and will appear in court today but it is a he, not a she."

"Are you telling me," Fletcher demanded as the potential of the situation dawned on him, "that you deliberately arrested an innocent woman?"

Then suddenly realising that a hole could be blown in his budget, he exclaimed in exasperation: "She can sue us for wrongful arrest!"

"I think that is highly unlikely," Amos replied calmly. "She will be charged with the equally unpleasant though lesser offence of blackmail.

The chief constable's jaw dropped. "Blackmail?" he gasped.

"Blackmail. It struck me as odd from the start of this case that a woman of apparently limited means, who previously lived in a rented flat in a rundown block, could suddenly afford to buy a luxury apartment. We don't yet know her original victim or victims but clearly she had put together enough cash by the time the refurbishment was complete and she naturally picked her old home, affording as it did an excellent view of the entrance to the block and others in the neighbourhood where she could keep an eye on various comings and goings.

"Quite recently she gained a hold over Jim Berry. He was desperate. He had already seen his life destroyed once when his business went belly up. Now he relied for a meagre living on Ray Jones, a born-again puritan who would certainly cut him off if he knew that Berry was being pressed to divulge his business deals so they could be sold to his rivals.

"Norman was threatening to shop Berry to the authorities for claiming social security without declaring his income from Jones. Poor chap. I doubt if he was earning over the limit that social security allows anyway but by this time

Berry was pretty unstable. He'd lost his firm, his wife and his wealth. He was eating too little and drinking too much. Norman pushed him over the edge.

"The night he murdered Jones by mistake he had sneaked into Killiney Court while the guard was round the back of the lifts smoking. He went up to Foster's rooms and gained entry, using a spare key he had been entrusted with when he was helping to rewire the block and had not bothered or forgotten to return.

"He took the duplicate set for the whole block that he knew Foster kept and removed the fuse for the lighting on the stairs, plunging them into darkness so he wouldn't be seen if he bumped into anyone.

"Berry then made his way upstairs. He knew the block had been renumbered, making the ground floor level one, but he hadn't reckoned on Foster's landing being counted as level two. Hence his foolish remark that all the residents thought they had gone up one level in the world.

"He let himself into Jones's flat in the dark and, knowing the layout of the identical apartments from working there, was able to get into the bedroom. With the curtains drawn there was just enough light to see a vague lump under the bed covers. Berry battered what he thought was the sleeping Elsie Norman, months of frustration and anger boiling over in the savage blows.

"Then he switched on the light. He probably intended to search for any incriminating evidence that Norman was using against him so that he could remove it. Imagine his horror when he found that the body he had savaged belonged not to his tormentor but to the man he saw as his benefactor, Raymond Jones.

"Berry fled, not even bothering to switch off the bedside light. He stumbled back down the stairs, returned the keys, restored the lights and slipped out before the errant guard had returned to his post.

"Worse was to come. Norman had photographed him coming into the block. They weren't very good pictures, taken through her window into poor artificial light, but you could just about recognise Berry.

"Little did Norman realise as she stepped up the pressure on Berry that he had actually come into Killiney Court that night to murder her, not Jones. She stepped up the blackmail and Berry, who was already under suspicion, feared the photographs would be enough evidence to put him in the dock for Jones's murder.

"Berry now had little choice but to lie low. Killiney Court was crawling with police for several days. Even after that we had a night-time presence in the building, mistakenly guarding Joanna Stevens. Besides, we were putting more pressure on Berry and he couldn't risk making a move."

"But what about the bundle of notes Elsie Norman gave him?" the chief constable butted in, finally finding his voice. "I thought <u>he</u> was supposed to be blackmailing <u>her</u>."

"On the contrary, the package contained prints of the photographs of Berry. When he heard that we had called off the inquiry, he was unleashed like a greyhound. I took great care that no-one would know I had removed Norman from the premises, not just to charge her with blackmail but for her own safety.

"I feel sorry for Berry. He has been dealt some pretty harsh blows in recent years – and I fear that I delivered the cruellest."

Rodney Hobson is a well-known journalist, author, broadcaster and columnist who has held senior positions in Fleet Street and in Asia.

His murder mystery stories, featuring Detective Inspector Paul Amos and Detective Sergeant Juliet Swift, are set in Lincolnshire in the 1990s in an area encompassing the Wolds and the Fens as well as the city of Lincoln. They are published as ebooks by Endeavour Press.

Rodney is married with one daughter. He is a member of the Crime Writers' Association, the International Thriller Writers and the Sherlock Holmes Society of London. He also writes on finance and his book *Shares Made Simple* is the best-selling beginner's guide to stockmarket investing.